C000000666

Granny Yaga
A Fantasy Novel for Children and Adults

VITALI VITALIEV

Copyright © 2014 Vitali Vitaliev

Front and back cover images © Sian Stocksley 2014
Illustrations © Sian Stocksley 2014

2nd edition 2016
All rights reserved.
ISBN: 1908756748
ISBN-13: 978-1908756749 (Thrust Books)

Reviews of Granny Yaga

"The kind of book publishers hate and readers love... the book is subtitled A Fantasy Novel for Children and Adults, raising such awkward questions as, "So is it for children or is it for adults?" The answer supplied by every beautifully crafted sentence may confuse some publishers, but it'll delight every reader: Granny Yaga is for the child in a grown-up and the grown-up in a child... The reader flies along with the narrative, never feeling like getting off, hoping the journey will never end and feeling sad that, like all superb books, it has to." *Alexander Boot, author, columnist and blogger*

"Delightfully inventive. Wickedly funny." *Marina Lewycka, author of* A Short History of Tractors in Ukranian

"A gripping read for all ages, from Danny's to Granny's." *Hilary Spurling*

"...His title, Granny Yaga, was enough to reel me in... Vitali is clever, witty and startlingly inventive... For those who like comic and clever fantasy, age irrelevant." *Herald*

"There are delightful elements to the novel; the cat with human qualities, the impact of questions, the reimagining of the old tales and characters. It's enjoyable... The British Museum is a key feature in the plot and I thought the curator who was particularly attentive to the reactions of his young visitors and took them seriously a nice touch, and different to the way museum curators are usually portrayed in fiction. It will be interesting to see whether the museum features in the sequels." *Kids in Museums*

"This book is unique. Read it out loud to your children, curl up with it on your own, present it to your young grandson and ask him to tell you about it - whichever way you take her in, Granny Yaga and her goings on will not only delight you but also teach you more about London and Eastern European folklore than anything else you'll ever read. The plot will captivate the youngsters, while the older reader will be left reflecting on who is in charge, the author or the characters, and how can the latter predict events the former hasn't even thought up as yet. Thoroughly recommended as an entertaining read for all ages." *Amazon reader review*

"An excellent and entertaining read from someone clearly immersed in the folk tales of his native land: Vitali Vitaliev - so good they named him twice. Bewitching… (Literally!)" *Amazon reader review*

"A wonderfully ironic and magic tale set in a beautifully researched layered London" *Amazon reader review*

"The book is framed as a fantasy but it also has a brilliant reality with stunning descriptions of London that capture the city as never before. There is no other book like this and as soon as my daughter hands it back I will be reading it again; perhaps like the author, in my shed." *Amazon reader review*

"A tale that can really be appreciated by young and old, with a truly lovable kid as the hero (not so easy to find) and the titular Baba Yaga as his Merlin." *Amazon reader review*

This book is dedicated, with love and warmest thanks

to Alina, Andrei, Anya and Mitya Vitaliev
who listened and encouraged

to John Hardress Lloyd
who guided and advised

to Christine
who supported and inspired

Contents

Prologue   1

Chapter 1
    In which we witness a series of bizarre events
    in Bloomsbury   3

Chapter 2
    In which we meet the Sablins and Danya finds out who his
    Granny really is   11

Chapter 3
    In which we learn about Yadwiga's past   23

Chapter 4
    In which Yadwiga becomes Baba Yaga and leaves the forest   33

Chapter 5
    In which little Danya visits Baba Yaga's Hut and meets
    her friends and servants, and his parents – five years
    later – go for a walk in London   41

Chapter 6
    In which Danya meets Bulgakov the Cat and the Sablins
    decide to leave Slavonia   51

Chapter 7

In which Danya gets a ride inside the mortar and his
parents get lost on the Tube five years on   63

Chapter 8

In which Danya and Olga explore their first English
garden while Yadwiga and their parents have their
first encounter with the police   73

Chapter 9

In which Sergei confronts football hooligans
and Yadwiga loses her flying kit   83

Chapter 10

In which Yadwiga clashes with Koshchei and wins   93

Chapter 11

In which the Sablins learn English by the "immersion
method", Koshchei poses as a female student and
Humphrey Smith gets a surprise delivery   103

Chapter 12

In which Danya visits the British Museum and
Koshchei comes up with a devious plan   117

Chapter 13

In which Yadwiga cracks Bulwer-Lytton's coded password
and Pani Czerniowiecka returns from the grave   131

Chapter 14

In which Yadwiga bumps into Bulgakov and his new
friends in a Crouch End café, the Sablins confront
Pani Czerniowiecka and Koshchei tries to use the
stolen password   145

Chapter 15
   In which Yadwiga and her friends continue their search
   for Lucinda, while Koshchei gets hold of the egg, but
   not for long   159

Chapter 16
   In which the sisters and the Cat travel to Brookwood   169

Chapter 17
   In which Yadwiga is reunited with her old flying kit,
   and Danya celebrates his eleventh birthday   179

Epilogue   193

From the Author...   195

About the Author   197

Granny Yaga in Auld Reekie: Chapter One   199

On seashore far a green oak towers,
And to it with a gold chain bound,
A learned cat whiles away the hours
By walking slowly round and round.
To right he walks, and sings a ditty;
To left he walks, and tells a tale...

What marvels there! A mermaid sitting
High in a tree, a sprite, a trail
Where unknown beasts move never seen by
Man's eyes, a hut on chicken feet,
Without doors, without a window,
An evil witch's lone retreat...

...There, in a mortar, onward sweeping
All of itself, beneath the skies
The wicked Baba Yaga flies;
There pines Koshchei and lusts for gold...

~

A. Pushkin, *Ruslan and Ludmila*

Prologue

FAR away and long ago... Well, actually, not that far away and not that long ago, twenty odd years at the most, there was a country ruled by evil self-proclaimed kings, or, as they called themselves, *tsars*, who could only be referred to as "great leaders," although in reality there was nothing great about them whatsoever. On the contrary, they were, in most cases, just dumb, and in the worst case – and most frequent – scenarios, both dumb and evil in how they treated their subjects, i.e. the people – like you and me. Yes, the people were pretty much the same as you and me, and I know it for sure because I myself had lived in that strange country for many years and am still seeing it often in my dreams. At times, in my dreams, it feels as if it is still here with us, and whenever I have a dream like that, I wake up in a cold sweat and can't go back to sleep for a long time... That country, which seemed both eternal and impregnable, collapsed suddenly, almost overnight – to everybody's surprise, as if some hidden magic power played a decisive role in its final demise. And who knows: possibly it did...

I don't feel like remembering my life over there too often, but at the same time, I don't want it to be forgotten completely, because if we forget, we can accidentally recreate it, so it is important to remember.

What was that country's name? I think most of you can guess. But even if you can't, it doesn't really matter, for that place is no more.

Let's call it the USELES – the Union of Slavonic Entirely Liberated Equalistic States, or Slavonia, just for reference.

And when it did collapse, there was a great feast, and the days went by with much feasting and drinking... I was there too, my dear friends, but the beer and the mead only wetted my non-existing whiskers – and not a drop ended up in my mouth...

The Writer

Chapter One

In which we witness a series of bizarre events in Bloomsbury

IT WAS a dark and rainy January afternoon in Bloomsbury, London. Victorian pubs around the British Museum were filling up with patrons. Tourists were flocking to the museum's courtyard and around numerous souvenir shops in the side lanes. Students from the newly opened Cordon Bleu Culinary Academy were leaving its freshly refurbished building in Bloomsbury Square.

At about five o'clock p.m., at the moment when the short winter day – bleak and brief like a final flash of a dying electric bulb – was about to be replaced by dusk and then darkness, a strange rider was seen galloping along the streets. His face was black, he was dressed in black, and he rode a coal-black horse. He galloped as far as the Russell Hotel and there, at the very edge of the Square, he suddenly disappeared, as if he had sunk into the ground. It was at that very moment that the night set in: the street lanterns lit up and the sky above London became dark... The pedestrians who spotted the rider all thought he was part of yet another touristy re-enactment – a hastily staged costume drama that had spilled out into the streets. Probably to publicise a new British Museum exhibition, or something of that sort...

A couple of hours later, Hooey Wong, a somewhat short-sighted Cordon Bleu Culinary Academy student from China, dropped her glasses case on the way out of the building. She bent down to retrieve it and while straightening up noticed from the corner of her eye a bizarre flying apparition in the dark sky straight above her head: a silhouette of an old lady in a red kerchief sitting inside what looked like an enlarged flying cocktail glass or a mortar (just like the ones they used in Basic Cuisine classes to prepare spices) and propelling herself forward with a thick mace-shaped stick resembling a large pestle... No one believed her when she later described the vision to her fellow students in the pub.

American tourist Map Halliday – from Texas – was standing in the queue to a British Museum exhibition with his wife Tommy. It was Friday, and the museum did not close until 8.30 p.m. Map was not sure what sort of an exhibition they were queuing for: something about pottery, or possibly about Islam – it was Tommy's wish to visit the famous museum on their last night in the UK. Bored out of his mind, Map was studying the early evening stars in the sky when he saw the quickly moving spectre of an old lady, with long matted hair bursting from under a red kerchief, above his head. Not very high, about 25 metres up. His pulled his wife by the sleeve: "Look Tommy, there's an old woman flying in the sky!" Tommy looked up, but saw nothing. "Grow up, Map!" she snapped at her husband. "You see goddamn women everywhere!"

Behind Map's back, at that very moment, Crispin Sneaky, a professional pickpocket, habitually working the Friday evening tourist crowd on the steps of the British Museum, quickly and almost imperceptibly rubbed his hand, with two outstretched fingers, past the Texan's bulging trousers pocket, pretending he wanted to squeeze past him up the stairs, but got distracted by the sight of an old woman in the sky holding something that looked like a police truncheon and waving it at him threateningly. Crispin's first thought was that it was a flying community police patrol... As a result, his practised hand, shielded by an empty plastic bag he was holding, trembled involuntarily and he missed the purse.

The only person who didn't get terribly surprised at the sight of the flying old woman was Humphrey Smith, deputy head of the British Museum's Pre-History Department. Detained at a long and tedious meeting about a forthcoming exhibition, *East European Folklore: Images and Symbols*, he was leaving via the staff entrance one hour later than usual. When he turned to close the door behind him, he was momentarily deafened by a brief and piercing yell: "Eeeeaaa!!!", right into his left ear, or so it sounded. He looked up and saw... well... we already know what, or rather, who... On coming home an hour later, he said to his wife: "Can you believe it, Sarah? As I was leaving work this afternoon, I clearly saw a pagan fairy tale character flying above my head and whistling into my ear!", to which his sober-minded wife replied: "You are working too hard, Humphrey. Why don't we both take a holiday as of next Tuesday and fly somewhere warm, like, say, Majorca, for a short break?"

The following morning, all London newspapers reported in chorus that on the previous night, a number of Londoners and tourists had become victims of "a collective delusion" and experienced "hallucinatory visions" triggered by the dour state of the economy and the most depressing time of the year. One tabloid went as far as to draw parallels with "a massive hysteria" in the aftermaths of Princess Diana's death.

* * *

That very evening, minutes after the events described above, there was a gentle knock at the door of Runes – a well-known Bloomsbury bookshop specialising in witchcraft, occult and the paranormal. Melissa, the shop owner, a buxom round-faced woman of an indefinite age, was about to lock up for the night. She was annoyed by this late visitor, most likely another tourist to ask for directions to the British Museum or to Buck House.

A very old dishevelled lady, with a long hooked nose and deep furrow-like wrinkles all over her face, limped in. She was clutching a black bin bag with some bulky, sharp-edged and heavy objects inside. With relief, she lowered the bag on to the floor, cleared her throat and began to chant in a creaky and sibilant, yet surprisingly energetic, voice:

"It was a dark and stormy night; the rain fell in torrents, except at occasional intervals, when it was checked by a violent gust of wind which swept up the streets (for it is in London that our scene lies), rattling along the housetops, and fiercely agitating the scanty flame of the lamps that struggled against the darkness..."

An experienced witch herself, Melissa immediately recognised the opening sentence from *Paul Clifford* by Edward Bulwer-Lytton. To most people, it was simply the notorious "world's worst opening of a novel", which had even triggered a jokey annual competition in America. But Melissa – unlike most – was well aware that this passage by Bulwer-Lytton, who was not just a famous and prolific Victorian author to rival Charles Dickens, but also a magician, known in the occult-leaning circles as The Wizard from Knebworth, was an international witches' password – a way of introduction and of greeting their own ilk. In the treacherous light of the dim energy-saving bulb of the politically correct "green" variety, she squinted at the intruder who suddenly looked very familiar to her.

"Yadwiga... Good Gardner! You have aged!"

"Little wonder," croaked the visitor. "People are too curious. They ask too many questions... You, on the other hand, have hardly changed in the last 600 or so years, or whenever it was that I saw you last."

"600 years! This cannot be true!" Melissa rolled up her eyes as if looking for something on the shop's ceiling, covered with crackles and brown spots left by water leaks. "Wait... We saw each other last much later, at the times of Tsar Ivan. He tried to catch us, remember, and even dispatched a unit of his *oprichniki* to the forest. They did capture me and made me work for the Tsar, but you and Lucinda escaped. That must have been less than 500 years ago! 600 years... That's much too long for sisters to be apart!"

"You may be right. My memory is not what it used to be, Melissa, dear. Nor is my magic, I am sorry to say. So much I have forgotten… Koshchei, on the other hand, is as nasty as ever!"

"He doesn't leave me alone either," sighed Melissa. "Not even here in London…" She stopped in mid-sentence, distracted by the sight of the bin bag at Yadwiga's feet. Its plastic flaps had fallen apart revealing what was inside.

"What's that sticking out of your bag? Good old mortar? I can't believe my eyes!"

"Questions, again!" Yadwiga grimaced. "Look at me: I am getting older by the minute! You'd better trust your eyes, Melissa. Yes, the mortar is a bit worn out – as any gadget would be after nearly a thousand years of service – and the pestle is slightly bent in the middle, but they are still an OK flying kit by all standards. We may be not as technically advanced there as you are over here, but we value good old things!"

"But, Yadwiga, this is junk that belongs in the museum across the road! Incidentally, they will have an exhibition of some pagan folklore-related items opening soon, so I would seriously consider donating your so-called kit to them! I myself fly the latest Dyson vacuum cleaner, with GPS and solar panels. It is almost noiseless and doesn't pollute the environment."

"Good on you, Melissa."

"And what happened with the Hut? Who is staying in it?"

Two direct questions in a row made Yadwiga wince as if from a pang of toothache.

"Please have mercy on me, Melissa, unless you want me to kick the mortar right here in front of you! I have recovered the Hut from Yesterdayland and brought it with me. Had to camouflage it as an old chest of drawers to smuggle it through Customs, and now I am trying to find a good spot for it in London – don't know where yet. Of course, I had to remove my lovely human skull–shaped lanterns to abide by the fire regulations, but otherwise all is in place, including Bulgakov the Cat – as naughty and as opinionated as ever before.

And my three faithful horsemen – Night, Day and Sun – are here with me too. All my servants are here, except for the pair of hands. They had got out of hand – forgive the pun – as of late, and stopped obeying me. Had to leave them behind, and asked Snake Horinich to look after them in my absence…"

Yadwiga paused and Melissa felt a sudden urge to embrace her long-lost sister.

"Sorry if I sounded smug," she said apologetically. "But I still have to ask you the main question. I won't say it aloud, don't worry, but you should be able to guess what I mean."

"You want to ask what has brought me here, of course. Well, I am going to tell you, but the answer may be too long to fit into this evening. So I will delay my white and red horsemen a little and slow down time, as one old *volkodlak* taught me ages ago. Ancient as I am, I can still remember how to do that, if only within a one-*versta* radius…"

Yadwiga lowered herself into a chair, snapped her long, crooked fingers and screamed loudly into nowhere: "*Yaghiyaghi chokh-chokh, mokh-mokh, ee-aa!!*" The bleak energy-saving light bulbs in the shop were suddenly replaced with heavy brass candelabra lit by dozens of burning candles. In their flickering light one could discern mottled cobwebs in the corners – which were clearly not there a second or so earlier.

Outside, in the back lanes of Bloomsbury, both cars and pedestrians slowed down to a crawl, like in a slow-motion picture. It took the publican of the near-by Museum Tavern over two hours to top up a pint of Guinness for a customer, who was incidentally no one else but pickpocket Crispin Sneaky, still shell-shocked by his vision of the flying police woman and seriously contemplating giving up his life of crime and signing up to a vocational training course in plumbing – the profession with much less risk and much higher takings than thieving. And next to him, Map Halliday, the tourist from Texas, all but froze over his tumbler of whisky and soda. His experience of a flying old woman in the sky and Tommy's crude reaction made him storm out of the British Museum courtyard and end up in this pub, where, over his second strong drink, he decided to leave his pushy wife with a masculine name and the manners of a professional baseball player, and start a new life in the UK. He had also decided to change his name to Atlas Halliday which would be his way of growing up, or so he thought…

Yes, everything and everyone slowed down inside the Museum Tavern – a famous Bloomsbury institution, once upon a time frequented, allegedly, by Karl Marx himself, but neither the publican, nor Crispin, nor Map (alias Atlas), nor all other patrons were aware of the delays, and the old Victorian clock above the bar kept ticking rhythmically – with 30-minute intervals between the ticks.

Back in the shop, Yadwiga and Melissa were sitting on chairs opposite each other in the Osiris position – their hands crossed over their chests, and their eyes shut – while Yadwiga's story was unveiling in front of them in real time – as if on a life-size 3D TV screen.

Chapter Two

In which we meet the Sablins and Danya finds out who his Granny really is

WHOSE Granny is she anyway?!"

Sergei Sablin put down the screwdriver, with which he was dismantling an old plywood wardrobe, and looked at his wife. "Didn't she come from that remote village in the north where your family has its roots? I remember her moving in with us shortly after we got married and were given this wretched communal flat… I also remember you saying we had to harbour the old woman because there was no-one left in the village to look after her…"

"You are right as always," Irina replied with sarcasm. "Only that God-forsaken little village had nothing to do with MY family. Miles away from where we used to live, it had always been your folks' domain!"

Sergei hated arguing with his wife. Firstly, because he loved her. Secondly, because she always won.

Like so many other long-suffering family women in their country, Irina was practical and full of common sense. Back in the Equalist times, common sense was about deciding if it was worth joining the seemingly endless queue for sausages, cheese, milk or, say, sweets which would take at least three hours of your precious after-work time, with the possibility that whatever you had been so patiently queuing for would run out the moment you approached the counter. It was also about balancing the meagre family budget in accordance with what they could afford this month: a new plain "business" dress for Irina herself (for her only other one was patched and getting threadbare to the point that it started provoking giggles from her male pupils and sardonic remarks from the headmistress), a decent "weekend" suit for her husband, a new pair of skis for their son Danya, or the simplest and cheapest CD player for their daughter Olga, whose only interests in life were boys and pop music, and her ideal pastime was therefore listening to boy bands which had just started appearing in their God- and Pop-forgotten country, where even the Beatles used to be frowned upon as yet another example of Western decadence and moral decay.

Irina's legendary common sense was also quite handy at work, because the subject she had taught at school – literature – was open to different and constantly changing treatments which solely depended on the differing and constantly changing attitudes of their country's constantly changing "great leaders". A classical character who was yesterday portrayed as a hero and an example for the young people to imitate in the literature manuals (these badly printed and dog-eared mass-circulation textbooks explaining the "true and only" political meaning of every single book, novel or story), today could be rebranded a "bourgeois", an "extra person" or even an "enemy of the people".

Irina Sablina, however, was adjustable and therefore had little problem keeping her pupils at work and her family at home under control.

It all changed with the collapse of the USELES (Union of Slavonic Entirely Liberated Equalistic States) and Equalism. Most people outside the Equalist Party elite and their relatives used to be poor as rats, now all of them – rats and people – were poor. Irina's teaching job was no longer enough to feed the family, so she found a new one as a cleaner in the house of a wealthy foreigner. At least – unlike in the Equalist past – foreigners were now allowed in Slavonia.

It had been different with Sergei, her husband, who worked as a technician (or as he himself used to say derogatorily, "a simple technician") at a large factory manufacturing primitive electric heaters, the so-called "reflectors", which didn't heat very well, and equally primitive refrigerators, which didn't freeze properly. These two main products of the factory could be easily swapped and interchanged with no-one noticing the difference. Nobody at the factory cared whether the gadgets they were making worked well, not-so-well or didn't work at all. The workers' and technicians' responsibility finished the moment another dodgy-looking gadget would slide off the conveyor belt. Selling them was someone else's problem, and using them was not a problem at all, for most of them didn't work anyway. At least they knew very well which brand of appliances to avoid having in their own households, if any.

As a rule, during the first three weeks of each month, Sergei was relaxed about his working duties, and most of his days were spent in endless "smoking" breaks in the company of his fellow workers (even though he didn't smoke). But the last week of the month was different. At the end of each month, government controllers would count the quantity of manufactured items and if it were lower than the accepted targets, it could negatively affect the workers' bonuses. On the other hand, if the targets were met or – in an unlikely scenario – exceeded, the bonuses would be safe. Not that the latter were significant – hardly enough for the traditional boozy end-ofthe month celebration – but losing them would have been a shame. Luckily, unlike the quantity, the quality of the factory's output was never an issue. It was not even considered by the controllers, simply because it didn't matter to them. This production "storming" reached its peak at the end of the year, when output would be the highest and quality the lowest. Everyone in the USELES was aware of that schedule and tried to stay away from anything made at the end of a month, let alone of a year. It was the same in each field and area: the end-of-the-year tractors, locomotives, saucepans, pencils, boats, buttons, tanks, handkerchiefs and spaceships were almost certainly defective and hence – if you could help it – not to be touched with a bargepole.

This "storming" nature of work could not fail to have a bad effect on the workers' character and self-esteem. And Sergei Sablin was affected by it too. A kind and gifted man, he had very little trust in himself and was totally reliant on his wife in running the family and everyday matters, particularly after the old Equalist system came to an end. The targets went up, the salaries down, and the whole factory was now owned by a foreign consortium – either Turkish or, possibly, Chinese, Sergei could never be sure. Luckily for him, the daily working routine stayed largely the same.

In short, both Irina and Sergei were in desperate need of some magic in their lives to make them bearable. But magic was well outside their reach. Or at least that was how it seemed until the sudden news of the demise of Irina's very old uncle, who had no other relatives and left everything he had – which was his spacious three-bedroom flat in a "posh" (by the USELES standards) suburb – to his niece. It WAS nothing short of magic – to be honest, Irina had only seen her uncle once, when she was still a little girl, and even of that one encounter she had a very vague recollection indeed.

The Sablins were of course all overjoyed, except perhaps for Granny Yadwiga, who knew much more about Irina's mysterious uncle than all of them together, and who was now following Sergei and Irina's argument closely from behind the tightly shut door of their room. No, she wasn't eavesdropping – just hearing every word clearly in her head. She was not worried about which of the Sablins won or lost, but simply – with one click of her fingers – made them completely forget about their little disagreement as to whose Granny she really was the moment Sergei picked up his screwdriver and resumed unscrewing the wardrobe's wooden legs one by one.

The Sablins' verbal exchange was also eagerly listened to by their ten-year-old son Danya, who was sitting at a small makeshift desk in the corner of the room pretending to be doing his homework. He didn't question Granny's murky origins, because – unlike his parents and his older sister Olga, who that afternoon was out with her friends, as usual, – he knew exactly where Yadwiga had come from.

He knew that his Granny was no-one else but Baba Yaga – a witch from ancient fairy tales – who joined the Sablin family when she could no longer live in the forest.

He found it all out by accident. In the true sense of the word.

It happened several years before, when Equalism was still running strong in Slavonia and Danya was still a very small boy.

The fruit on the blue plate looked fresh and yummy. A large pink apple was surrounded by shiny hillocks of green and red grapes, their succulent oval berries reflecting the sun. The rim was lined with strawberries, and the remaining spots were covered with fiery – as if sun-drenched – mandarins and small lemons resembling clots of condensed summer daylight.

Little Danya could stare at the fruit plate for hours when in bed. It wasn't hard, for the magnificent, mouth-watering display was hanging on the wall of the lounge, which also doubled as Danya's and his parents' bedroom, right under the ceiling. Why the fruit was suspended so high and how it was managing to stick to the vertical surface of the plate and not to fall down was anyone's guess. Danya preferred not to think about it. He already knew that too much rationalising and too many questions could not just spoil the fun, but could also be dangerous.

Wasn't it what his parents and his Granny Yadwiga meant by advising him repeatedly to hold his tongue and never voice what he thought without thinking about it first? To think before thinking? How foolish was that!

And that other silly adult expression: "Walls have ears." No matter how hard Danya searched the walls of his bedroom-cum-lounge, no matter how thoroughly he groped them, there were no signs of any ears growing through the wallpaper, not even in those multiple spots where it got unstuck from the wall to reveal bald patches of peeling stucco.

It would have been nice, he thought, to find somewhere on the wall a pair of pink piglet's ears – for some reason, he was sure that the wall's ears, if any existed, should resemble those of a pig, stirring and rotating, like two tiny radars, as if conversing with each other.

The fruit on the plate, however, was better than the ears on the wall. And there was no need to look for it. Here it was – high above Danya's head – in all its saliva-inducing beauty.

In reality, fruit like this could only be bought at the nearby collective farm market, which used to be called the peasant market before Equalism, when instead of collective farms there were just peasants, as Granny Yadwiga, who was very old, told him. Danya liked going to the market and watching the loud-mouthed, moustached fruit-sellers in flat "aerodrome" caps, which made them look like oversized mushrooms, promoting their goods by shouting and calling out to everyone, including children: "*Daragoi!*" – which in their peculiar language meant "darling." The prices of their fruits were so forbidding that even Danya's parents, who both worked, let alone Granny who didn't, could not afford them.

Well, to be fair, there were times when one could buy fresh fruit and veggies in normal street shops, like the constantly empty Tempo food store in their street, and even from some stalls and kiosks. For two weeks in June, fresh strawberries were on sale everywhere, but after that they would magically disappear from view (and from shops, if not entirely from market stalls) until the following June. The same was true with watermelons, Danya's favourite fruit, albeit he had heard from someone that watermelon was actually not a fruit but a berry, the only difference being that they would start turning up in kiosks on street corners in late August and would vanish by the end of September. Together with apples.

Bananas were simply unheard of and, as for citruses, as adults referred to oranges, lemons and mandarins, in their part of the world they were as rare as snowstorms in the Sahara Desert.

That was how Danya's ordinary year could be painted, with pastel spells of strawberries, apples and watermelons and long and drab fruit-less gaps in-between – not too colourful a palette.

Potatoes were the only natural product they were never short of, not even in winter. Danya would have been amused to learn that the French called potatoes "apples of the earth." Every autumn – normally in early October – Sergei would take Danya with him to his factory to pick up their family's winter supply of potatoes. Nearly every organisation provided several bags of that essential staple for its employees at reduced prices – depending on the number of "mouths" in the family. During winter, the bags were routinely stored in apartment block cellars, or – if there were none – in some dark corners of communal kitchens, bathrooms and even toilets.

Danya loved those annual potato expeditions for which his Daddy would hire a wobbly, ancient truck. It was fun riding back in its warm and cosy cabin , which smelled of petrol and tobacco smoke, bouncing on road bumps and talking to an old, as most adults seemed to Danya, driver in a leather jacket who treated him respectfully – as if he were a grown-up too.

Going down to the cellar to fetch potatoes in winter was less exciting. It was a bit scary. Not that Danya any longer believed that a Baba Yaga – an old hook-nosed witch from fairy tales – was living in the basement, as he did a couple of years earlier. He simply disliked the all-permeating damp and the pitch darkness before his Dad switched on a weak, naked, solitary bulb. Its uncertain glow seemed not to generate light but to create shadows, and the sight of the cold rotting potatoes, with worm-like white spikes protruding from them, making them resemble some dirty small porcupines piled up in the basement corner, was altogether not particularly enticing.

Now you will understand why the plateful of permanently fresh and exotic fruit was such an attraction to Danya. The fact that it was suspended from the ceiling well out of his reach only strengthened his craving.

On that day, the desire to taste the forbidden fruit became totally irresistible – largely due to the fact that Danya was "sick" in bed and didn't go to prep school. Why did I, the Writer, attach quotes on both sides of the word "sick" – like hooks to a painting or a fruit plate before it is hung on the wall – you may ask? And my answer will be: "Because Danya wasn't really ill, but just pretending!" It was easy and only took complaining of feeling unwell in the morning and then rubbing the mercury-filled thermometer tip against the blanket when his parents looked the other way – and bingo: the magic 37.1 degrees! Anything under thirty-seven was considered "normal" and therefore "school-able", yet one had to be careful not to overdo the rubbing and end up with forty-three – the temperature at which the human heart may stop beating.

Danya needed those breaks from his school's strict routine whereby all kids had to wear grey uniforms made of rough ticklish cloth. They were expected to sit at their desks with their arms neatly folded and were only allowed to talk after raising a hand and being invited to do so by the teacher.

On the other hand (which didn't even have to be raised!), while "sick" in bed, he could read, browse through his dog-eared "Atlas of the USELES Railways" and imagine himself on all those trains, play with his toys and look at the mouth-watering pictures in his favourite volume of all, *The Book of Healthy and Wholesome Food*, which – just like all other books – started with a quote from one of the Great USELES Tsars: "One of the peculiarities of our revolution lay in the fact that it gave the people not just freedom but also material well-being and the possibility of a plentiful and cultured life."

And although Danya could understand little in that quote, it didn't stop him from enjoying the detailed masterful drawings of food and drink, most of which he had not only never seen, but never heard of: smoked salmon, champagne, caviar...

For about ten minutes, Danya had been staring at the fruit plate while drumming on the back of his nickel-plated bed with his index and middle fingers to imitate rattling of train wheels: *ta-ta-tata, ta-ta-ta-ta* – his favourite sound. Then he made a final appraisal of the situation and decided that the moment had come.

The Sablins lived in a one-room flat, if not to count the common – or communal – kitchen, bathroom, toilet, the conveniences they had to share with three other families – and a seemingly endless dark corridor. Granny Yadwiga had her own curtained little corner in the middle of that corridor, where she slept on top of a huge and permanently locked antique wooden chest of uncertain origins and purpose.

Yes, the moment was right: Danya was now alone in the flat - his parents were at work, his sister Olga at school, and as for Granny Yadwiga, she was too busy in the communal kitchen a long way down the corridor cooking her signature dish, potato pancakes.

Having climbed out of the bed, Danya pushed two chairs underneath the fruit plate, lifted one – with an effort – and placed it on top of the other – with an even bigger effort. He then quietly pulled in a round piano stool from the corridor. Due to the absence of a piano in the communal flat, the stool was used by male tenants as a prop for brushing and polishing their shoes before going out.

Having rolled up the sleeves of his pyjama top and the trouser legs of his long, much too long, pyjama bottoms, Danya stepped onto the seat of the lower chair tentatively with bare feet, while grabbing the back of the upper chair with his hands. The whole structure was unstable and very wobbly, but there was no going back for Danya, driven not so much by his desire to taste the fruit as by sheer determination, better known as stubbornness.

He climbed onto the seat of the second chair and straightened up his legs while holding on to the piano stool and trying not to look down. Another pull up – and Danya's tummy was resting on the stool's round seat. The challenge now was to stand up again – and then the magic blue plate would be well within his reach.

Danya bent his knees preparing to make his torso vertical. As vertical and straight as possible. It was not easy, for now his hands had nothing to hold on to, except for the stale – almost palpable – air of the room: Granny was suffering from a persistent fear of draughts.

Waving his hands in the air like a rope walker, Danya attempted to stand up without losing his balance. And nearly succeeded. Nearly. In his far-reaching plan, he forgot to take into account one significant detail: the seat of the piano chair was a ROTATING one. The moment Danya straightened his legs; the piano chair started moving underneath them...

It was like in a slow-motion pantomime of which Danya himself was the sole actor and spectator. He could feel the ground disappearing from under his feet. The coveted plate was close to his face, yet Danya realised with sudden clarity that he was not destined to reach it. Not this time, at any rate... In a last desperate effort, with the flimsy chairs-and-stool barricade collapsing underneath him, he jumped up in the air and tried to grab the pink round apple with his open mouth, but failed – only his front teeth scratched the apple's skin a little as he fell...

Even as he was falling down, Danya had time to realise that the apple was not real. Just like the whole tacky display on the plate and the plate itself, it was decorative and made of wax. He also realised that he was about to hit his head against the sharp protruding corner of his and Olga's makeshift desk, crudely assembled by his Dad from boards, planks and pieces of wood he had covertly brought home from work. Danya closed his eyes and could not see Granny Yadwiga flying into the room and grabbing him tightly by the waist the moment his temple touched the corner of the desk.

When he opened his eyes, they were both up in the air: he in Yadwiga's arms – hovering in circles under the ceiling and then landing smoothly on the chipped parquet floor.

"Go back to bed, you little mountain climber," croaked Yadwiga and shuffled towards the door.

"Wait, Granny, wait!" Danya screamed. "I didn't know you could fly! You are also so strong... Who are you, Granny??"

Yadwiga turned back sharply: "I hate being asked questions! And I will tell you why: each question makes me a little bit older than I am already – and you would find it hard to believe HOW old. I will be one thousand and forty-seven years old this coming Sunday, believe it or not. But on this occasion, I will forgive you. I will also tell you who I really am, but only if you promise not to tell anyone, under the peril of something truly horrible happening to you and your parents."

"I promise, Granny! I promise!"

Yadwiga sat on the edge of Danya's narrow bed and started her story.

Chapter Three

In which we learn about Yadwiga's past

HUNDREDS and hundreds of years ago, in place of the vast and modern country called Slavonia, with all her cities, motor cars, gangsters, spaceships, oligarchs and ice-breakers, there was just an enormous thick forest, surrounded on all sides by a no less enormous Wild Field.

The forest people, to whom Yadwiga belonged, were called the Krivichi. Some of them lived in small wooden huts, others in dug-outs, warmed up in winter by fires. These fires were kept burning day and night, for the Krivichi did not know how to start a fire and their biggest fear was that all the fires in their land would be extinguished by wind, rain or snow and they would be left in permanent cold and darkness. The punishment for allowing a fire to go out – either by negligence or by carelessness – was severe. That was why they worshipped Perun – the god of thunder and lightning who could start a fire literally out of thin air during a thunderstorm. It was then the Krivichi's task to keep it alive for as long as possible.

Another big threat to the Krivichi and their fires came from belligerent tribes of nomads who populated the Wild Field: the Khazars, the Polovtsi and the Pechenegs. Unlike the Krivichi, who hadn't yet tamed horses, the nomads were excellent riders and merciless fighters too. The forest people always lived in fear of their sudden devastating raids, when many of the Krivichi men would be killed and women tied to the saddles and taken as trophies to the nomads' camps to lead lives of misery and servitude.

While boys and men spent their days hunting and fighting, women took turns looking after the fires, and as a young girl Yadwiga would often sit awake throughout the night – staring at the hearth and adding logs to it, while knitting or weaving, and struggling not to fall asleep.

Young Yadwiga liked looking after the burning fire and working at a simple wooden spinning wheel: *Ter clack! Ter clack!* The rhythmic sound of the wheel was soothing and a little soporific too. One night, exhausted after a full day of berry picking and lulled by the monotonous sound – *Ter clack! Ter clack!* – she dozed off for an hour or so and stopped adding logs to the fire. She woke up with a start. It was pitch dark in the dug-out: the fire had gone out.

Soon all the other dug-out dwellers woke up cold. They now had to send envoys to the neighbouring tribe – the Drevlianie – and try to borrow fire from them. That could take several days during which the Krivichi had to stay in cold and darkness and to survive on berries, herbs and mushrooms.

To punish Yadwiga, three of her fellow tribesmen wrapped her tightly in a bear's skin and carried her to the thickest corner of the forest where she had to stay until the end of her days in the company of eleven other young women, all guilty of a similar negligence. Very few of them were destined to live through winter, for how can you survive bitter wind and frost without fire?

It was because of the poor state of their health that they were all known as *yagishnas* – from the old local word *yaga*, which meant "illness".

Most of the girls had already spent months in the thicket, where they all shared a crude wooden hut. They were all weak and pale, yet they met the newcomer warmly. Well, with as much warmth as they could summon up from their shivering bodies and desperate souls. Despite all the ailments they were suffering from, each of the *yagishnas* had her own special gift: one – whose legs were too weak for walking – had learned to move around and even to fly using some simple kitchen utensils, like a pestle and mortar; another was able to predict the future; another one was such a marvellous story teller that her tales came alive and dragged all the listeners into them, as if they were all integral, yet invisible, characters in the narrative. The girls spent countless evenings in their hut listening to the stories and trying to warm themselves up by imagining they were all sitting around a burning fire.

On one particularly cold night, a lonely traveller knocked at their door. He was tall and although in excellent health, he was extremely, almost inhumanly, thin. Unsurprisingly, his name was Koshchei, which in the old Krivichi dialect meant "skeleton". He told the girls he was a *vezhlivets* (a sorcerer whose aim was to protect the young from disease and the evil eye) and a magician who could give them fire, but there was a price for that: instead of twelve *yagishnas*, they had to shape themselves into just three. Not that nine of the girls had to die for the remaining three to survive, but rather, as Koshchei himself explained, all of them would have to merge together and then split into three new entities, each of whom would be a superior person – a deathless super-human to rival Koshchei himself in her magical powers.

The girls were all so cold and miserable that they agreed immediately. Koshchei ordered them to jump into a huge cauldron full of cold water. Then – with a simple click of his long worm-like fingers – he started a fire underneath it. The last thing Yadwiga could remember was feeling pleasantly warm for the first time in many weeks. Then there was darkness…

She woke up on a soft green lawn. It was summer, and the sun was shining in her face. The forest was full of light and life, and she could hear birds chirping cheerfully above her head… She knew she was still Yadwiga, but not her former exhausted self. The new Yadwiga was full of oomph. She felt so strong and vigorous that she wanted to fly.

Next to her on the lawn two other girls were waking up. Their names were Melissa and Lucinda, and although they did not resemble each other a lot, they decided they would now behave like blood sisters: live together and support each other as much as they could.

With time, it transpired that Koshchei was right: each of the three sisters had inherited some of the twelve *yagishnas'* peculiar magical skills and qualities, but there was one that all three of them shared – they were immortal and so, just like Koshchei, were destined to live forever.

Each of them had a special gift of her own. Melissa was particularly brilliant at the magic of transformation. Nothing was impossible for her: she could easily turn into any living creature – from a tiny mosquito or a bird to a bear, yet, unlike Koshchei, she was unable to transform herself into inanimate objects, like a knife or, say, a saucepan. Lucinda's main strength was in seeing the future. She knew exactly what was going to happen the following day or week: when heavy rain or snow were about to fall, so that the girls could make sure in advance that their precious fire was safe, and when the next Polovtsi raid was likely to happen to give the sisters ample time to hide in the forest. She could also see much, much farther ahead, and that was probably why she was generally quiet and taciturn, at times completely withdrawn from reality, so powerful and absorbing (or perhaps incomprehensible and scary) was whatever she could see in the future… As for Yadwiga, she willingly took charge of the three magic Horsemen: red, white and black – who represented the sun, the day and the night. They became her most faithful servants, and with their help she was able to slow down or, if necessary, speed up the course of time. Once a year, she would split herself into three separate *yagishnas* – in her case three "Yadwigas", who existed simultaneously in three different places and three different times – tens, hundreds or even thousands of years apart. But that last transformation could not continue for more than one day at a time.

The girls were leading a very good life in the forest. They built themselves a cosy log cabin and adopted a stray black cat whom they called Bulgakov, after a famous writer of some very distant future Lucinda had once managed to get a peek at. They also tamed a fire-breathing, yet nice and kind, three-headed dragon, whom they jokingly nicknamed Snake Horinich – from the verb *horit*, "to burn". Since then keeping the fire alive stopped being much of a problem, for Horinich could always rekindle the dying flames with his fiery breath.

Soon, rumours of the three beauties living deep in the forest spread all over the Krivichi land and beyond. People were curious to see for themselves. Every day dozens of visitors knocked at the door of the girls' house under different pretexts: to ask for directions while pretending to be lost, to borrow the fire, or just for a friendly chat, if not with one of the three *yagishnas*, then with their loquacious and philosophically learned Cat. Children wanted to stroke Horinich the Snake and to feed him logs, or to fetch a ride inside a magic mortar.

The sisters were suddenly busy receiving visitors day and night and had no time left for themselves. They decided to take precautions: they hired a pair of human hands to help them with house chores and to scare off some particularly noisy and nosy intruders during the day. And at night the house was guarded by human skulls with burning eye-holes stuck on top of the fence. When even that did not prove sufficient to keep gapers at bay, a pair of live giant hen legs were attached to the foundation, so that the Hut could turn around to face the *yagishnas* and away from an unwanted visitor at the sound of the magic mantra which only the girls themselves and their most trusted friends knew: "Hut, Hut! Stand with your back to the forest, your front to me!"

Entrance to the sisters' house during the day was made conditional on the visitors being assigned such seemingly impossible tasks as carrying water in a sieve and washing a couple of frogs.

Inevitably, disappointed people who had failed to gain access soon started spreading all sorts of nasty rumours about the girls: that they were all vicious witches, or *ved'mas* (from *ved'ma* – "the one who knows" – in the local tongue) and cannibals, with hooked noses and iron teeth and with a particular taste for little children. The girls would laugh off these rumours in the beginning, but then decided they could be useful in bringing them some coveted peace and quiet and stopped denying them actively.

The *yagishnas'* most frequent visitor – who, with time, became their biggest scourge and nightmare – was Koshchei himself. He always appeared unannounced and demanded attention. Koshchei thought the girls should be eternally grateful to him for freeing them from their miserable, disease-ridden and fire-less existence, whereas in fact the sisters hated him for his boastful arrogance and for taking nine of their friends away.

With time, Koshchei started showing special preference for Yadwiga. Old and ugly as he was, he could still be romantic at times and would appear on the girls' doorstep in the guise of a young and handsome prince, with colourful hair ribbons or other nice gifts for all three sisters and a bunch of fresh field flowers especially for Yadwiga. Yet Yadwiga remained indifferent to Koshchei's advances until the following episode.

One day, an angry and heavily armed knight invaded the sisters' territory in the middle of the night. Having failed to persuade the Hut to turn its front towards him (for he didn't know the magic mantra), he started scouring around and found the flying mortar and pestle hidden in the bushes. He broke the pestle in two against his knee and then chopped the mortar into small pieces with his battle axe. Encouraged by his achievement, he retraced his steps towards the Hut, having failed to spot how the pieces of the broken pestle and mortar raised themselves from the ground and stuck back together behind his back, without a single trace of breakage. That very moment, Yadwiga, who had been woken up by the noise, stepped out onto the porch of the Hut to see what was happening. Hiding from the skulls' burning light, the knight crawled up to the porch and grabbed Yadwiga from behind. He took out a short and crooked nomad's sabre – a trophy from a recent clash with the Polovtsi – and was about to cut her throat when Koshchei suddenly fell from the sky and touched the knight's head with his index finger, at which point the knight's whole body froze and turned to stone. He then took Yadwiga in his arms and carried her inside the house.

With time, more details emerged about that episode which, as it turned out, had been completely set up by Koshchei, who first kidnapped the poor knight's wife and then, having disguised himself as a clairvoyant vestal, told him it was Yadwiga, the vicious *ved'ma* living in the forest, who had captured his wife and was keeping her prisoner in the Hut on chicken feet. But Yadwiga knew nothing about it then, and even her sister Lucinda was unable to enlighten her, since she could see the future, but not the past.

This is how Koshchei found a way to Yadwiga's heart. Soon they started living together in Koshchei's castle on top of a large rock overlooking the sea. Yadwiga left everything she had to her sisters, except for the flying mortar and her three faithful Horsemen – Day, Night and Sun – who refused to be left behind and followed her to Koshchei's tsardom. But even they were too much for Koshchei, who wanted to have full power and authority over Yadwiga. He was jealous of her ability to speed up and slow down time and of her immortality, which Koshchei thought only one creature in the whole world had the right to enjoy – himself.

As a result, he treated Yadwiga very badly and forbade her to leave the castle while he was away carrying out his dark mission: inciting people against one another by making them miserable and greedy.

But with her old mortar and pestle at hand, Yadwiga started sneaking away to see her sisters, always trying to be back in time for Koshchei's return. One day she got delayed playing with Snake Horinich and trying to pacify Bulgakov the Cat, who was missing her terribly and complained of being depressed and generally disappointed by the futility and pointlessness of his feline existence. How could she abandon the poor pet without listening?

When she returned to the castle, Koshchei was already home and fuming with rage. They had a row after which she got into her mortar and flew away, and Koshchei chased her through the sky as he was (he did not require any aids or gadgets to fly), the flaps of his black-spider-dotted nightgown flying in the wind.

Yadwiga finally landed on a moon-lit lawn, with Koshchei dropping down from the sky a second later.

"You want to leave me," he croaked. "OK, I don't mind. May the road seem a tablecloth to you! I have always lived on my own and will keep doing so until I die. And I will never die, do you know that? It is not for nothing that they call me Deathless. But before I let you go, I will punish you for your ingratitude. I am going to take away your immortality. You are still going to live for a very long time, but one day you will die. Unless I die before you, and I am Deathless!!"

"Why are you doing this to me, Koshchei?" asked Yadwiga, and – to her horror – the moment she uttered these words, she could feel the first wrinkles forming on her face, above the eyes. She ran to a nearby stream, knelt and – when the full moon peeped out briefly from behind the clouds – looked at her reflection in the dark mirror-like water. It was true: her face appeared a tiny bit older.

"This is what's going to happen every time you ask a question and every time you are asked one too!" laughed Koshchei. "So you'd better keep your curiosity in check. As for your sisters, I could easily do the same to them, but they haven't upset me as much as you did, so I'll keep them immortal and will punish them in another way."

"Do anything you want to me, but leave Melissa and Lucinda alone!" Yadwiga pleaded. "They haven't done anything to you, Koshchei. But if you still dare, I'll find you and will have my revenge, for I know you are not entirely deathless. Lucinda, who can see through time, told me that your death is on the top of a needle inside an egg inside a duck, and whoever breaks that needle will kill you!"

"He or she will have to find it first, ha-ha-ha!"

With a coarse, bark-like laugh, Koshchei levitated briefly above the lawn, then shot up above the trees and disappeared in the clouds.

Shocked and confused, Yadwiga sat on the wet, cold grass all night, listening to the soothing murmur of the stream and feeling lonely and abandoned by everyone, until her faithful friend – the White Horseman – rode past her on his snow-white stallion.

Dawn was breaking slowly, as if reluctantly, above the trees.

Chapter Four

In which Yadwiga becomes Baba Yaga and leaves the forest

I T WAS only when the Red Horseman galloped through the meadow and the sun started rising above her head that Yadwiga stood up and slowly walked back to the Hut.

She could see from afar that the skulls were no longer on top of the fence. They were scattered all over the lawn like oversized pine cones, and their eye-holes were black and light-less. The door to the Hut was wide ajar and everything inside was upside down. Her sisters were nowhere to be seen.

From behind the stove, Bulgakov the Cat limped out. He told Yadwiga that a unit of *oprichniki*, the Tsar's secret policemen, had raided the house during the night. They came to arrest the three *ved'mas* on the orders of the Tsar. Lucinda, who had had a bad premonition the day before, had enough time to use her magic: she climbed onto the roof through the flue, turned into a white dove and escaped. Melissa was grabbed by the hair, tied up and blindfolded before she could even click her fingers. They took her away. Snake Horinich tried to free her, but lost one of his heads in the fight that ensued and retreated to the forest to heal his wounds with flowers and herbs and wait for his head to grow back. Bulgakov himself had managed to hide behind the stove where the *oprichniki* could not reach him.

"The policemen kept saying to each other that they needed to catch all those sorcerers and witches or risk the Tsar's wrath," recalled the Cat.

It was the start of a big and cruel witch hunt in the aftermath of a huge fire in the Krivichi's main settlement in which many people had died. The fire was of course started by Koshchei, but the Tsar was led to believe that the three forest witches were to blame and ordered them – and all other *ved'mas* in the land – to be captured and killed. On the same night that Yadwiga left Koshchei, all Krivichi women who were not married and lived on their own were arrested and thrown to prison. They soon went on trial to determine whether they were witches or not, and most confessed to being ones under torture. Those who didn't confess were tied up and tossed into a pond or a river. If they didn't drown, they were proclaimed *ved'mas* and burnt at stake. If they did, well... then they were declared innocent and buried.

Melissa was lucky, for the Tsar himself took a liking to her. He freed her from imprisonment and made her a nanny to his young son. When the boy was in his teens, Koshchei had him killed and made it look as if the boy's father himself was the killer. No-one, however, was prepared to accuse the Tsar of a murder, so Melissa was blamed instead. She had to flee hastily and did not return to her homeland ever again. That was a timely escape, for Koshchei soon took full control of the country, renamed it Slavonia and made himself its next Tsar. He ruled Slavonia for many hundreds of years under the guises of different tyrants: the Viking, the Boat Builder, the Liar, the Doomed Boris, the Big German Lady (yes, Koshchei could assume the looks of a female too!), the Liberator, the Peacemaker, the Healer (the latter was not actually a proper Tsar but still had all the power in the land), the Weakling and many others.

Under the Weakling's rule, there happened a turmoil, during which Koshchei briefly lost power to the Lawyer, who was a decent man and didn't know any magic – black or white. He didn't last long. Koshchei quickly restored his authority by having the Weakling executed and forcing the Lawyer to flee the country dressed in woman's clothes. He then carried on with his black magic dictatorship well into modern times, calling it Equalism. Slavonia was duly renamed the USELES – the Union of Slavonic Entirely Liberated Equalistic States – and Koshchei kept ruling it as the Lisper (together with the Pole, his main prison warden and executioner), the Murderer, the Peasant, the Medallist, the Oldie, the Spy, the Tongue-Tied, the Drunkard, the Puppet and finally the Wrestler. And although there were exceptions, some of the qualities of all those rulers remained unchanged over centuries (no wonder if we remember they were different incarnations of one and the same creature – Koshchei the Deathless): they were all ruthless, could lie through their teeth without blushing or feeling any shame, were extremely selfish and cared only about themselves.

As for Yadwiga, after the hut was raided, she hastily relocated to the remotest corner of the forest, where she built a new – smaller – Hut on chicken's legs, and stayed put for several hundred years, only occasionally receiving visitors who arrived by accident. A *berehynia* by nature (a hearth mother and protectoress of the home), she was always nice to her guests and asked for just one thing in return for her hospitality – to spread horrible, scary, at times bordering on ridiculous, tales about her and her sylvan abode: that her nose was so big it grew into her Hut's ceiling, that she cooked children in the oven and ate them for supper, that she had bony legs and iron teeth, was a champion snorer, could inflict a *porcha* (disease) on everyone, and so on and so forth. She wanted to be left alone so as not to have to ask any questions or be questioned herself. The gullible people must have enjoyed being scared: they swallowed everything, even the clearly idiotic and meaningless mantra: "Fee – Fi – Fo – Fam – I Can Smell Human Blood," which Yadwiga herself invented, with some help from Bulgakov. With time, she became known as Baba Yaga (the *Porcha* Woman): parents were scaring their children with her ("If you don't behave, Baba Yaga will come, take you away to the forest and eat you up!"), and her name alone made people tremble with fright.

In a way, Yadwiga had achieved her goal, for one normally doesn't question the object of one's fear but runs away instead. She thought that if she managed to remain in relative solitude (her servants and Bulgakov didn't count), she still had a good chance to live a very, very long life, even if not an eternal one, like Koshchei and her missing sisters, of whom, incidentally, absolutely nothing had been heard. With time, she found out from a visiting *vestalka* (clairvoyant) that Melissa had a base somewhere in England, but that was all she had managed to learn. As for Lucinda, her whereabouts remained a total mystery.

And that was how she lived for several hundred years: picking berries and mushrooms or flying high above the earth in her mortar during the day, and – on seeing the Black Horseman – staying inside her Hut to listen to Bulgakov's readings and never-ending laments. Or, having teamed up with one of Snake Horinich's heads (all three of which were back in place by then), playing a simple card game of *doorak* (fool) against his two remaining heads, who usually won.

She didn't know how many years had passed. Koshchei seemed to have left her alone, and she was happy in her own way, if missing her sisters.

Everything, except for eternity, eventually comes to an end, and the time came when Yadwiga's life in the forest became at first difficult and then outright impossible. With the Murderer in power, everything in the land, including the ancient forest, was suddenly subject to "industrialisation". Unable to motivate the people to work hard and produce enough food for themselves, the Murderer resorted to threats and repressions, and his successor, the Peasant, ordered every single patch of land – be it woodland, rocks or even town streets – to be ploughed and planted with maize, for one of his courtiers, a quack and a charlatan scientist, assured him that maize was both nutritious and easy to grow anywhere. Lumberjacks were dispatched to the forest where Yadwiga's Hut stood, and the great "deforestation" began. Yadwiga shuddered when she first heard that horrible tongue-breaking word which gave you a headache when pronounced.

With Snake Horinich's help, she first tried to scare the lumberjacks, but failed: they were permanently drunk and were inclined to dismiss the sight of her whooshing above the tree tops in a mortar or that of Snake Horinich's three fire-breathing heads as alcohol-induced hallucinations, which they called "white hotties," and kept drunkenly chopping off trees (at times their own hands and fingers too) for all they were worth.

She even tried to charm the lumberjacks into submission by appearing on the porch of her Hut naked – without realising that her looks were not what they were five hundred years earlier. Her long hair was no longer ginger and no longer fell down her shoulders like a small waterfall, but was grey and matted; her skin had largely lost its smoothness and was wrinkled and dry; her nose, which had never been small, had now become very long and crooked; most of her once white and sparkling teeth had fallen out, and a couple of crude replacements, made of tree bark, were sticking out of her mouth like some rotten dark brown claws... It was only Yadwiga's eyes, deep green and hypnotically bottomless, that remained young and beautiful.

Her appearance on the porch in the nude, however, did bring Yadwiga a temporary respite. Only instead of being "charmed" by her wild beauty, as she had hoped they would be, the lumberjacks – drunk as they were – had the scare of their lives. Having thrown down their saws and axes, they ran away squealing with fear and shouting: "Baba Yaga! Baba Yaga!!" (*Porcha* woman!)

They soon returned, for their fear of the supreme USELES ruler, be it the Murderer, or the Peasant, proved much bigger than that of Baba Yaga and Snake Horinich combined. The forest was getting thin and threadbare, and one morning Yadwiga woke up to the loud buzzing noise of a mechanical saw – a fresh innovation of the Murderer's court engineer. The moment she heard that horrible sound it seemed to be ripping her whole being apart, as if it were she, Yadwiga – not a hundred-year-old pine tree in front of her Hut – who was being mercilessly dissected by the rotating blade.

The last drop – literally – came when a flock of flying metallic monsters dived out from under the clouds one morning and began spraying the newly-made maize-planted clearings and the few remaining bits of the forest with some sticky foul-smelling liquid which made Snake Horinich, whom Yadwiga had sent to intercept the intruders, choke and throw up smouldering coals from all his three mouths. It made Yadwiga sick and dizzy too.

The omniscient Bulgakov claimed the smelly liquid was called "fertiliser" and the process of spraying it from the air "fertilisation".

No matter what it was called, Yadwiga knew it was time to go. But where to? The forest was no longer safe, and there wasn't much left of it anyway... After a lot of thinking, Yadwiga decided that the safest place for her to hide would be in a town, among people. She knew she was different inside, yet on the face of it she looked unremarkable: an ageing and slightly stooping – she finally had to face the truth! – little lady with a kerchief covering her curly grey hair. In the streets of a town she would resemble a typical countryside Granny visiting her grandchildren. And that was the image she eventually decided to adopt.

But which family to choose? She was waiting for a sign to point her in the right direction. While perusing the scanty ads page of a local newspaper (the USELES rulers did not approve of any private ventures, including personal advertising) she had picked up while flying above an empty town very early one morning, she came across the following: "A working family of four are looking for a live-in nanny for their little boy. Please call and ask for the Sablins."

When Yadwiga saw the last name "the Sablins", she immediately knew it was the sign she had been looking for. Her most precious charm was the crooked sabre, or in the old Krivichi language *sablia*, of the confused and aggressive knight who nearly cut her throat with it hundreds of years ago and which Koshchei had allowed her to keep. Yadwiga had treasured it since then and kept it in a safe place next to her most valued possessions: a tin with the "water of life" from the very cauldron where she and eleven other *yagishnas* were boiled into existence (a couple of drops were enough to bring a person back from the dead), and her magic wand, which she seldom used, for she also had magic powers in her fingers. She thought the sabre, or *sablia*, was meant to bring her the good luck which she so desperately needed. Yes, dear readers, the truth is that witches and magicians are in need of good fortune too, for this is one thing no magic is able to achieve. A good spell can make you happy for some time, it can even make you rich, but no sorceress or magician in the world can make you lucky. Being lucky is something which is either there or not there, and no-one knows exactly where and how it happens.

Life in the forest had taught Yadwiga to be cautious so, before contacting the Sablins, she decided to watch them for a couple of days. She liked Sergei and Irina immediately: hard-working, kind and intelligent people living in a tiny one-room flat and struggling with the gruesome realities of their daily existence. She was unsure about their daughter Olga, who appeared superficial and self-obsessed, but Danya, the little boy, won her affection immediately. When semi-jokingly threatened by Sergei, his father, with Baba Yaga, who "will kidnap you and take you to the forest unless you calm down and go to sleep this very moment," the boy said defiantly in a high-pitched and sonorous voice: "But I am not afraid of Baba Yaga and want to meet her!"

She phoned the Sablins, got the job and moved in with them the following day. The only thing she had brought with her was a heavy wooden chest. Yadwiga explained to the Sablins that she kept all her worldly possessions in it and that the chest could also double as her bed, if they gave her a bit of space in the communal kitchen or in the corridor, to which the Sablins and their neighbours readily agreed. Irina donated an old patchwork quilt to be placed on top of the chest instead of a mattress. Little did the Sablins know that inside the chest was a dark portal leading to Yesterdayland and to the last remaining patch of the forest in which Yadwiga's Hut on hen's legs was still standing and where her trusted friends and servants – Bulgakov the Cat, the three Horsemen, the skulls and the pair of hands – were always waiting for her. And outside the Hut, hidden under a thick branchy bush and guarded by three-headed Snake Horinich, was her flying kit: mortar, pestle and broom (the latter to sweep away her traces in the sky) – all ready to be used.

After a couple of weeks with the family, Yadwiga decided that her choice had been right. She made the Sablins quietly forget about her being a nanny (that was a very simple spell) and start regarding her as a "Granny" instead.

Chapter Five

In which little Danya visits Baba Yaga's Hut and meets her friends and servants, and his parents – five years later – go for a walk in London

LITTLE Danya was mesmerised by Yadwiga's story and still a bit dizzy from their joint flight under the ceiling. He wanted to ask Granny so many questions and had already opened his mouth to utter the first one when he remembered her Koshchei-imposed predicament and simply said: "Thank you, Granny."

"I bet you are dying to shower me with questions," smiled Yadwiga. "I will try to preclude some of them. And to thank you for your modesty and good behaviour, I am now going to invite you to visit my Hut. It is time to feed Bulgakov anyway. That Cat is so lazy – he never bothers to catch a mouse, but just sits on the stove all day and reads clever books: Jung, Montaigne, Bulwer-Lytton… I've also got a treat for Snake Horinich – a litre of high-octane petrol for each of his three heads. Petrol for them is like vodka for a drunkard. Or like soft ice-cream for you, he-he-he…"

"But how…" Danya began, but cut himself short. "Sorry, Granny…"

"Please watch it, Daniil," Yadwiga wagged her finger. "Every 'how', 'what' or 'when' means another wrinkle on my face – even if the question is not complete!"

"One day when I grow up I will find the egg with Koshchei's life in it and will free you from this curse!" Danya said emphatically.

Yadwiga was touched by his words, but chose not to show it.

"You obviously wanted to ask how we were going to get there," she smiled. "It is not such a long journey. Just get off the bed and follow me!"

She shuffled out of the room, and Danya – in his pyjamas – went after her into the dark communal corridor. None of their neighbours seemed to be at home: they were probably still at work or on trams held up in traffic on their way back home.

There, in a small alcove near the coat hanger, stood Yadwiga's old chest. She lifted its heavy lid with effort and peeped inside. "I wonder what the weather's like down there today," she mumbled. "I should probably put on a shawl or something warm. And you should wear a sweater on top of your pyjamas – just to be on the safe side, you know."

Danya ran back to the room and returned wearing a sweater.

"Just do exactly as I do and don't be afraid," said Yadwiga.

She climbed inside the chest and invited Danya to join her. He didn't have to be asked twice.

"Now, hold on to me tight!" Yadwiga clicked her fingers and uttered in a loud whisper: "*Yaghi-yaghi chokh-chokh mokh-mokh eeaah!!*"

Danya could feel his feet falling through the cold wooden bottom of the chest which suddenly disappeared and revealed a black and seemingly bottomless abyss, into which he and Yadwiga were being sucked by some mysterious and powerful force. In a moment, they were... not falling, but rather floating down, like two autumn leaves, big and small, through a black chilly void which smelled very much like the Sablins' potato cellar – of mould, damp and rodents' droppings. Their descent lasted no more than thirty seconds – and here they were, lying supine on a soft grassy lawn, looking at the pale end-of-the-night stars above their heads. In no time, a dark shadow fell on their faces and blocked the view. It was Snake Horinich hovering above them like a curiously shaped giant kite.

"Yadwiga is here! Wake up, Bulgakov!" all his heads screamed together, having revealed three oven-like mouth cavities, with bright flames dancing between sharp and long teeth like bonfires. To

Danya's pleasant surprise, the dragon did not look scary. On the contrary, considerable warmth was oozing from all his six eyes, as if they were indeed heated up from underneath by the flames in all his three mouths.

"Welcome, Danya, to Yesterdayland and to our forest, or rather to what remains of it," said one of the heads.

"Before you ask the question, I want to explain where exactly we are," Yadwiga said to Danya. "Some years ago, when my life in the forest became unsustainable, I decided to move the Hut and the small allotment around it to Yesterdayland, where only those who could travel back in time would be able to find it. I have also arranged for my servants to stay there indefinitely. As for myself, due to old Koshchei's curse, I can only spend three hours at a time in Yesterdayland, or else I lose the ability to return to Today. And, frankly, more than once I've been seriously thinking of retiring to Yesterdayland forever – that was before I met you and your family, of course. Here I would have been safe from lethal questioning, but would probably very quickly die of boredom instead... So let us hurry, Daniil: we don't have much time left."

Yadwiga helped Danya get up from the grass and, having squeezed his soft little hand in her dry bony palm, led him towards the Hut, no more than a couple of hundred yards away. Danya could already discern its silhouette, lit up with multiple red lights.

"Now, Danya, time for you to be brave," said Yadwiga. "You are about to see my lovely human skull lanterns and to meet my extra pair of helping hands. A couple of things to remember: do not stare at the skulls straight in the eyes, for they will burn you down to ashes within seconds. And do not under any circumstances shake either of the helping hands. They will be all over you, like two puppies – and this is fine: they are playful as well as hard-working, and they like visitors. But for Krishen's sake, don't let them shake your hand, when they try to do so, unless you want to become what they are – just a pair of hands without a head and a body!"

At this point, little Danya felt like freeing his hand from Yadwiga's grip and running away. Or at least ask Granny a myriad of questions. But he did neither and, towed by Yadwiga, kept approaching the Hut.

He found avoiding the skulls' eyes easy and was already hoping that the hands would not notice him, for how can they, with no eyes and ears, he was thinking, when he suddenly felt a gentle whiff of air on his cheeks, as if a bat had just flown straight above his head. In fact, not one bat, but two human hands severed at the wrists were fluttering around him like two large butterflies, or indeed like bats, with their outstretched fingers resembling membranes. Danya didn't notice how one hand descended to his tummy level and tried to grab his free right hand (his left one was held tightly by Baba Yaga). Having sensed the icy fingers' touch, Danya withdrew his hand hastily.

"Get lost, you headless loiterers, and leave the boy alone!" Yadwiga shouted at the hands and waved her fist at them. The hands obeyed immediately. Having flailed briefly above Danya and Yadwiga, they flew towards the nearest tree and hid themselves in the foliage.

"They have a nice and warm nest in that tree in an old mitten of mine," Yadwiga explained and added: "Don't worry, they won't come back."

They continued their progress towards the Hut. In the left-hand corner of the courtyard Danya spotted an oblong wooden building. A warm pinkish glow was emanating from its puny mica-covered windows and from the door that was half ajar.

"These are the stables where I keep my three beautiful horses: black, white and red," said Yadwiga. "Time in Yesterdayland is different to that of Today. It is late at night here now, and my black horse is out in the forest with its night-time rider, but they should be back soon – and then it will be the white one's turn."

The Hut was now in front of them. It was a log cabin with a triangular chamber-style roof and a small smoking chimney made of bricks. At first, Danya thought that the Hut was levitating a couple of metres above the ground, but then he noticed two very large hen's legs with long sharp claws sticking out from underneath the house, like stilts. These clawed stilts seemed alive and were shifting from one to the other, as if impatient or wanting to pee, and because of that the Hut itself was swinging gently back and forth, as if trying to warm itself up or dancing.

Danya squinted at the Hut, but could see neither a porch nor a front door, just a wall made of rough thick logs.

"Not a nice way to meet the mistress, but security is paramount these days," Yadwiga grumbled. "Now, Daniil, you should know the magic mantra from your fairy tale books. Do try and make the house turn, if you can."

Of course, Danya knew the mantra! How could he forget it?

"Hut, Hut! Stand the way your mother placed you – with your back to the forest, your front to me!" he cried out.

For a second or so, the Hut stopped swinging and stayed motionless, as if straining its invisible ears (and Danya knew from his parents that walls COULD have ears!) to hear the command properly, then – with a high-pitched squeak that sounded more like a squeal – started turning around slowly on its two giant legs. Having completed a 180-degree turn, it came to a stop, its ornate little porch and its neat front door facing the newcomers.

"Home at last!" declared Yadwiga. "Let's get inside!"

* * *

At this point, let us interrupt Yadwiga's story and our own truthful narrative just for once – and, having left Yadwiga and Danya on the porch of the Hut on chicken's legs, check on the Sablins five years later. For that, we'll have to leave Yesterdayland and briefly return to the present.

On the same long evening that grew into morning when Yadwiga was telling Melissa her story inside the Runes bookshop, a curiously dressed couple could be seen walking in Elm Tree Wood, which, in all sincerity, was not a wood, but a small public park in a quiet middle-class suburb in North London. Unlike some pedestrians in Bloomsbury, they were well outside the one-*versta* range of Yadwiga's slowing-down spell and were therefore walking at a normal – not snail's – pace. For the end of January, the weather was mild, with the temperature well above ten degrees, yet the woman was wearing a long and heavy artificial fur coat of the type that is always full of static electricity and can give one a mild electric shock when touched casually in a crowd. And if rubbed thoroughly for a minute or so, it could perhaps spark off a small bonfire... The man's coat was lighter – of a simple cotton and wool variety, but on his head he was proudly sporting a *shapka* – a massive black hat with ear flaps that gave the wearer a friendly Cocker Spaniel-ish look. To relieve the worries of some animal rights activists and to activate the concern of others, we hasten to add here that the hat was made not of dogs' fur, but of rabbits'.

As some of you may have guessed already, these two overdressed morning pedestrians were Sergei and Irina Sablins on their first ever London stroll. As for their fifteen-year-old daughter Olga, she staunchly refused to leave the house, where she had been watching television from morning till night while looking after her ten-year-old brother Danya. The latter didn't feel like going out either, but he wished even less to be looked after by Olga whom he had come to dismiss as shallow and uninteresting. And although at fifteen Olga had full legal right to be left alone with a younger sibling (Irina had checked the relevant UK regulations), since their arrival in London the Sablins had tried not to leave the children on their own, not even for a minute. This time, however, they deliberately made sure Danya and Olga were not accompanying them on what they claimed was just a "leisurely walk" in the park (there's nothing quite as boring for kids as a "leisurely walk"), but was in actual fact a very focused and purposeful expedition in search of the nearest job centre.

They had been put up at the house in Woodville Avenue by Yadwiga, who claimed it belonged to an old friend of hers, a Polish lady called Pani Czerniowiecka, or – to use an anglicised version of her name – Ms Black, who was away temporarily. It was a seemingly unremarkable two-storied terrace house, with a large garden at the back and a smaller one in front. Yet the house had a couple of special features: inside it was very Victorian, bursting with antiques – old furniture, mirrors and lots of useless trinkets on mantelpieces above countless fireplaces – all in good working order. Outside, on the roof of what used to be a small gardener's bedsit, was a red sculpture of a dragon which some passers-by were inclined to regard as a symbol of Welsh-ness. They would have been very surprised had they found out that the sculpture had nothing to do with Wales and that it wasn't even a sculpture, but a living dragon, albeit a very quiet, taciturn and patient one, who could remain completely motionless and hence sculpture-like for weeks and even years as he was guarding the house at 125, Woodville Avenue.

The street itself was nice and neat, bordering on posh. The only house that stood out was number 127, next to the Sablins' new abode. It was extremely neglected: with cracks on the walls, a moss-covered roof and a front yard overgrown with weeds and bushes. In the middle of the front yard, half-hidden under the foliage, sat an ancient dumped car – an early 1930s Morris, with a peculiar number plate – "AER 8". It looked as if it had been out of use for decades, and grass was growing not only from under its long-deflated wheels, but from its sagging and rusty roof too.

It was obvious that Sergei and Irina had misjudged the severity of the London winter – so much milder than their habitual snowy one back in Slavonia. By the time they entered Elm Tree Wood and were passing by a secluded ivy-covered cottage behind a tall fence, they were both sweating profusely.

"What a strange little house!" exclaimed Sergei pointing at the cottage. "It belongs in the middle of nowhere, not in the centre of London!"

"Well, first of all, we are not quite in the centre of London," interrupted Irina who liked precision in everything. "And secondly, I find this little cottage rather cosy, much more so than the old pile with a dragon on the roof found by Yadwiga. I can't even start to think what kind of rent her Polish friend is going to ask for!"

Sergei took off his rabbit-fur hat and wiped his forehead with a hanky.

"You should be ashamed of yourself, Ira," he said. "Didn't you hear Yadwiga saying that her friend had allowed us to stay there for free? Until we find jobs, that is. And look what a great area we are in: it feels like a dream after Slavonia!"

At that point, Sergei spotted a large black cat's head above the cottage fence. The cat's green eyes stared at him with almost human intelligence and with considerable curiosity too. Even if the cat was standing on his hind legs, he was still huge. Unless of course he was supported by some invisible prop behind the fence, or simply stood on a ladder.

"Look, Irina," Sergei said to his wife pointing at the fence. "Have you ever seen a cat as big as that?"

Irina looked in the direction of Sergei's outstretched hand, but saw nothing. "I can't see any cats or dogs for that matter," she said ironically. Sergei turned around: the space above the fence where the giant cat's head had rested a moment ago was blank. He thought he must have experienced a momentary hallucination – the result of a bad, fitful sleep the previous night.

"Sorry, Ira," he said. "Let's move on."

They stopped again briefly near a small children's playground, next to which stood an oblong and windowless Victorian building, which looked like an abandoned barn or a hangar. It appeared to be under some sort of restoration, of which it was in desperate need: uneven, flimsy and apparently unreliable scaffolding (probably put together in haste) could be seen on one of its sides. The purpose of that massive Victorian pile was a mystery, but one thing was clear: it was totally out of place and out of proportion in Elm Tree Wood.

At this morning hour, there were no kids in the playground: only a couple of business-like grey squirrels were sitting at both ends of a bulky wooden see-saw and rubbing their little paws together – as if rejoicing at being alive.

"I do like this area, Sergei," Irina said to her husband. "And you are right: anything would look like paradise after the USELES. But I am worried as to how we are going to survive here in the West. Who is going to give us jobs when we cannot speak a word of English? I am too proud to ask for benefits from the state… And what's going to happen to our children? They have already missed a lot of school. For how much longer can they waste their days watching television?"

"Let them watch it," Sergei puffed out. He was now unbuttoning his coat. "It may help them to pick up English faster. Children are better with languages than grown-ups, don't you know that? As for us, we ARE going to get some work soon, I am sure. I would do anything: stack up shelves in a supermarket, clean toilets – anything at all. After the nightmare we had to go through in Slavonia, any menial job would be a blessing. Besides, Yadwiga promised to help us."

"Yadwiga? Don't make me laugh! She is just an old lady. And a foreigner here as well. What sort of power can she have?"

"She may indeed be an old lady, but she is not as simple as you think," said Sergei as they resumed walking across the park towards the main road exit. "To begin with, she is already fluent in English. And don't forget, it was Yadwiga who had found us the place to live and who had helped us leave Slavonia. Sometimes, I even think there's much more to her than just an old Granny…"

"Of course, she is much more than that," agreed Irina. "She is in some ways very modern. Despite her ancient looks… Also she absolutely adores the children."

"Not so sure about Olga, but she certainly worships Danya," said Sergei as they left Elm Tree Wood, crossed the busy High Street at the pedestrian lights and went inside an Underground Station for their first ever London Tube journey.

Chapter Six

In which Danya meets Bulgakov the Cat, and the Sablins decide to leave Slavonia

IT WAS dark inside the Hut. Dark and warm. The ante-room smelled of dried herbs and log fires. The door to the *gornitsa*, the Hut's "clean part", was shut. Yadwiga opened it – and Danya was momentarily blinded by the bright fluorescent light.

"Forgot to warn you about the light," Yadwiga mumbled. "The Hut is powered exclusively by Yesterday's unused energy – and there's plenty of that, as you can imagine."

A large part of the neat and brightly lit *gornitsa* was taken up by a tiled stove. A massive oak table and four solid chairs stood in the middle of the room. The table was covered with a vast starchy tablecloth, hand knitted and embroidered with sophisticated flowery patterns.

"Take your seat, Danya," said Yadwiga, pointing at one of the chairs. "And tell me what you feel like eating: the journey must have made you hungry."

"I'd love an ice-cream, Gran, but you probably don't have it, because I cannot see a fridge... so don't worry."

"Of course I have it!" Yadwiga croaked. "I have everything you can think of: caviar, sturgeon, fresh lobsters – you name it! Well, if I were able to pose questions, I would now ask you about your favourite sort of ice-cream perhaps..."

"Er... Vanilla and strawberry would be great!"

Yadwiga clicked her fingers, at which point the four corners of the knitted tablecloth went up and joined together in the middle, forming a parcel. In a second or so, the cloth unfolded to reveal a crystal bowl full of white and pink balls of ice-cream.

"Enjoy!" said Yadwiga. "And don't forget to say thank-you to my self-cooking *samobranka* tablecloth! Saves me a lot of time, although once in a while I like to cook myself, using my programmable Aga oven, the only one in the whole of Slavonia. Trust me; I cook proper meals, not poor little children – as so many people seem to think. No *ved'ma* in her right mind would want to eat naughty little brats who would only give you heartburn and indigestion. And after a nice home-cooked supper, I relax with my self-playing psaltery which knows all my favourite tunes."

Danya was so busy with his ice-cream that he didn't notice how a very large black cat appeared from behind the stove. He was walking on his hind legs while his front paws were clutching a book.

"Meet Bulgakov," Yadwiga said to Danya. "He has been with me for over seven hundred years since that day my sister Lucinda and I found him as a stray kitten in the forest. A fine cat he is, but a bit lazy: he loves nothing better than lying on the stove with a book."

"Books are a source of knowledge!" the Cat said authoritatively. He had a pleasant tenor-like voice.

"Knowledge..." Yadwiga repeated sarcastically. "I am all in favour of it, but it can also be dangerous. As they used to say in the good old times, the more you know – the sooner you die."

"Sorry, Yadwiga, but I have to disagree with you," said the Cat. "Just listen to this." He opened the book he was holding and read aloud with obvious pleasure:

The wide recognition accorded to such books shows that there must be some supra-individual quality in this image of the anima, something that does not owe a fleeting existence simply to its individual uniqueness, but is far more typical, with roots that go deeper than the obvious surface attachments that...

"Bulgakov, enough of that!" interrupted Yadwiga. "We have a child here, and the works of Carl Gustav Jung might be a bit too adult for him, as you should have guessed! Jung was a good man who treated magicians with respect and wanted to become one himself, but never quite made it. I used to tell him often: 'Try to be less complicated, Carl. Forget all this scientific nonsense and get down to basics.' But he wouldn't listen."

"OK, let me try something else," said Bulgakov. He was already holding a different book in his paws. It was a dog-eared old folio which had just one word – *Zanoni* – printed on its cover in large and partially faded golden letters.

It is possible that among my readers there may be a few not unacquainted with an old bookshop, existing some years since in the neighbourhood of Covent Garden ... there, perhaps throughout all Europe, the curious might discover the most notable collection ever amassed by an enthusiast of the works of alchemist, cabalist, and astrologer...

At this point, Yadwiga interrupted the Cat again.

"Bulgakov, I know you are doing it deliberately, knowing how much I miss my sister," she said and explained to Danya: "I haven't seen my other sister Melissa for nearly six hundred years – since the day she fled Slavonia and settled in England. For quite some time I didn't feel like getting in touch with her, thinking that the memories of our past life might be still too fresh and too unsettling for her after just three or four hundred years. But, as recently as one hundred and seventy or so years ago, I asked my friend and fellow magician Lord Lytton of Knebworth, who was also a famous writer, to trace her down covertly, which he did. It turned out she was running a magic bookshop in London, and inside that bookshop there was..." She suddenly stopped in mid-sentence, then continued: "Never mind what was in it – you may find out one day, but Lord Lytton, whom I used to call simply Edward – and still do – chose to write about her shop in one of his numerous novels. It was pretty mean of you, Bulgakov, to choose that particular book now, when we are in a hurry. Look, it's nearly morning, and my three hours in Yesterdayland will expire soon!"

"Please accept my apologies," said the Cat. "But I simply can't let you go before you listen to something special I have just discovered."

"As you know, Danya," he carried on, addressing the boy, "books do not just allow us to travel back in time, they can also open up the future. Here in Yesterdayland, we live in the past, but to keep us properly balanced, we are given the ability to read books of the future – the books that not only have NOT been published yet, but that may not have even been written yet! And this particular one might be of interest to you both."

He lifted his head and gave out a long loud hiss. A hardback appeared in his outstretched paws – literally out of nowhere.

"Here we go. *Granny Yaga* by Vitali Vitaliev," Bulgakov read from the cover. "It will be written in 2012 and published in 2014 – and all of us are in it, including myself, believe it or not! There's one particularly important life-changing episode here that happens exactly five years from now."

Yadwiga and Danya were unable to contain their curiosity. They sat down on a crude wooden bench near the stove and prepared to listen.

It was the morning the Sablins had been waiting for. All their possessions had been packed in crates and boxes, and several pieces of furniture, including Danya's little desk, Olga's CD player with stereo speakers, Sergei and Irina's wardrobe and Yadwiga's chest-cum-bed, were wrapped up in old rags and blankets, ready to be loaded onto a removal lorry, which had been booked for 8 a.m.

Yes, today they were leaving their cramped bedroom-cum-lounge in the communal apartment, with its long dark corridor, its shared bathroom where three wooden toilet seats – one for each of the sharing families – were hanging on the walls like oversized and totally luckless horseshoes, and its cockroach-ridden kitchen, smelling of cabbage soup and rotting potatoes. They were moving to a much bigger "separate" flat, left to them by Irina's newly deceased uncle. It was located in a prestigious, if not to say posh (for "posh" did not really exist in Slavonia – not in the Western sense of this word) part of the town, populated by high-ranking officials, ex-Equalist party bureaucrats and other influential crooks. It has to be said that, unlike their parents, neither ten-year-old Danya, nor his fifteen-year-old sister Olga were looking forward to the move, because it implied changing school, which in turn meant saying goodbye to their friends and facing the need to make new ones – not an easy task in the notoriously exclusive and hence probably stuck-up area to which they were now moving. As for Granny Yadwiga, she was not feeling too well that morning: she had a splitting – in the true sense of the word – headache that normally preceded her annual split into three *yagishna* entities which at times stayed within the same space and time parameters, yet occasionally were capable of existing simultaneously in three distant and totally different countries and eras before merging back together in a day or so.

The removal men were unusually punctual – only one hour late – and, even more unusually, only slightly drunk. Having received a ten-*dengas* donation (read bribe) for tea (read vodka) from Irina, on top of their "official" fee, they began loading their battered van reluctantly. There was not enough space in it for the Sablins themselves who had to make their own way to the new apartment. Olga suggested a taxi, at least for the women, to which Sergei grudgingly agreed (it is not every day that you move your family to a new flat, after all), but insisted on Danya and himself taking a tram which was a practical decision (as well as a gentlemanly one, that is), for the teeny USELES-manufactured cabs were only capable of carrying four passengers max.

A holy place is never empty – as an old Slavonian proverb goes – even if it is not a whole apartment, but just a one-bedroom communal flat. With the severe housing crisis, a permanent feature of both the Equalist USELES and post-Equalist Slavonia, the moment the Sablins drove off, another removal truck carrying their room's new tenants' furniture pulled over ready to be unloaded.

It took Sergei and Danya several hours to get to their new area of residence: first, there were no trams at all for nearly an hour, then they started arriving in flocks of three and four, but none was the one they needed. At some point, their tram – number four – did appear in the distance, yet when it was just a mere fifty yards away, something extraordinary happened: the carriage stood stationary for a second or so, then started crawling back and away slowly, as if drawn by some kind of invisible giant magnet, and soon disappeared from view!

It was probably the only case of a tram going backwards in the whole history of Slavonia. Sergei and Danya could be forgiven for thinking that some magic force was trying to stop them from reaching their new place of residence (and, in actual fact, it was!).

When, at last, their tram did arrive, it was a decrepit jalopy – a wobbly, rusty and squeaky cart on wheels, that was probably already in use during the reign of Tsar Ivan.

It was a slow and bumpy ride. Every couple of minutes the tram would grind to a halt at a set of forbidding traffic lights that seemed to display three variations of one and the same colour – red. During one such stop the driver entered the salon to announce that there was no power in the overhead cables, so everyone had to get off. At that point, Sergei was secretly grateful to Slavonia's erratic electricity supply for interrupting their seemingly endless tram journey and giving him a valid excuse to flag down a cab.

They finally reached their destination a couple of hours after the women. Looking back at that particular point in time, Sergei would often wish they never did. He saw all their meagre possessions, gained by years and years of hard work, scattered all over the pavement, next to the doorway of their new block of flats. Although, as it quickly transpired, the flat was actually NOT theirs. It had been firmly occupied for over a week by one of the country's new rich who had made an office in it.

In vain did Irina wave all the ownership papers in the ruddy and beefy faces of the oligarch's body guards, or whatever those square-shouldered and heavily armed men were – they seemed to be in possession of their own papers and warrants, all duly stamped and signed and all stating unequivocally that the apartment belonged to a certain Citizen Koshkin, not to the Sablin family. And when Irina tried to protest, the square-shouldered guards – or whoever they were – simply pushed her aside and ordered the removal men to dump all their cargo onto the pavement and get lost. Just like Danya before his plunge into Yadwiga's magic chest and from there to Yesterdayland, the removal men did not have to be asked twice. Particularly when they saw a couple of blunt shotgun muzzles aimed at them at close range. They promptly got into their van and disappeared liked greased lightning.

That was the situation Sergei and Danya faced when they got out of the taxi: Irina and Olga crying over piles of their belongings, and Granny Yadwiga – looking lost and absent-minded – sitting on the ground under a tree with her head in her hands and mumbling something incoherent which sounded like *"OM MANI PADME HUM,"* or a similar abracadabra, which made Sergei think that she had either already lost her mind or was about to do so.

"Wait here and don't move!" he said to Danya and, jumping over their own overturned chairs and tables, dashed towards one of the apartment block's gaping doors only to be stopped and pushed back by a burly-looking guard with a Kalashnikov across his chest.

"I want to talk to your boss, I want to talk to Citizen Koshkin!!" Sergei was shouting.

"Stay away, if you want to live," the guard barked out before stepping back inside the black hole of the doorway.

"Sergei, stop it, leave them alone!" screamed Irina. "Think of our children!! Let them have this damned flat. We can always come back to our old one…"

"No, we can't, Ira, we can't! That's the whole point. We have signed it off and the new tenants have already moved in. We are homeless!"

"It's better to be homeless than dead, Sergei… Let's go!"

"Where to?"

"Anywhere. Away from this place! Danya, Olga, come on. And where is Granny? She was here a minute ago suffering from a migraine... Oh, here she is, poor thing – hiding under the tree. Stand up, Gran. We have to go!"

They all trudged towards the nearest militia precinct. Knowing how corrupt those guardians of law and order were under Equalism, and how much more corrupt they had become since the USELES' collapse, the Sablins did not cherish a lot of hope of getting any help there. And they were right. A fat vodka-reeking militia Major in a soiled black uniform laughed in their faces and told them that their papers were fakes. "The crook who gave them to you should be p-prosecuted," he stuttered. "Or maybe you have faked them yourselves?" He could not wait to have this annoying family, with their constantly moaning little Granny, out of his hair. "The apartment lawfully belongs to Citizen K-Koshkin and no-one else!" he concluded sternly.

The moment Yadwiga heard the name "Koshkin" she knew what was going on. "Koshkin" was one of Koshchei's favourite reincarnations, which sounded similar to his name, yet not quite the same. It was his way of scaring her away by reminding her who she was dealing with. And, in this particular case, he succeeded: not only was Yadwiga too weak and poor to fight Koshchei in the middle of her splitting-up cycle, but even in the prime of her youth and in the best of her health she had always found it hard, if not impossible, to repel his black spells. The truth was that – evil as he was – Koshchei still remained the world's most powerful magician. And he was never going to forgive her for rejecting him. In short, on this occasion, Yadwiga was unable to help the Sablins. The only thing she could do was move away and take the family with her.

There was a small littered park next to the militia station. And that was where – in an empty children's playground – the Sablins ended up after their brief encounter with the Major. Sergei and Irina were straddling opposite ends of a rusty see-saw, Olga settled herself on a squeaky swing, and Danya sat astride a battered wooden horse. He was holding a toy cardboard steam engine which he and Sergei had put together only several days earlier with glue and scissors – the only "possession" of theirs, if not to count the contents of their pockets and the clothes they were wearing, that the Sablins had managed to salvage. Yadwiga was nowhere to be seen, and they all thought she was still on her way – plodding ahead – and would catch up with them any moment.

Trees were rustling above their heads, and some invisible birds were chirping in the bushes. There wasn't much to say.

"We must get out of here!" Sergei breathed out suddenly.

"Out of where? This park? This area? This town?" asked Irina.

"This country! This cursed and ungrateful country where we don't have any future!"

He was waiting for Irina to object, to start an argument, probably even to insult him for being so impressionable and stupid.

"I think you are right," she said quietly. "We've just been spat in the face by the system. We must leave… but where shall we go? Who needs us?"

"Let's go to America!" Olga called out from the swing. "They have Hollywood, Disneyland and cool cars!"

"This is crazy, Olya. Who is going to give us the visas?"

"How about England?" They didn't notice how Granny Yadwiga appeared in the playground. It was obvious she didn't have a headache any more. She straightened up, and her whole posture conveyed strength and determination. She even looked younger than an hour ago, or so it seemed.

"How about England?" she repeated in a loud and confident voice. Her splitting-up day was the only time of the year when Koshchei's curse had no effect, so she could ask questions, and be asked them too, without getting older.

"It is a great country, but balanced." she carried on. "It has always harboured those who were badly treated in their homelands. Besides, we have relatives there…"

"Relatives in England? What are you talking about? I've never heard of them. Had the USELES authorities known about it, we'd all have been in trouble," said Irina.

"I have two sisters whom I haven't seen for donkey's years," explained Yadwiga, "and I have reason to believe that at least one of them lives in London. I can get in touch with her – and she would send us an invite."

"But this will take ages!" Sergei exclaimed. "Don't you know how notoriously slow Slavonian bureaucrats can be? Where are we going to live in the meantime? And where will we get the money to bribe them all into giving us permission to emigrate?"

"I have thought about it all," Yadwiga answered mysteriously. "It may not be as long as you think."

"England…" Irina uttered dreamily. "Shakespeare, Dickens…"

"Sherlock Holmes!" intervened Danya.

"Take That, X Factor, Girls Aloud!" added Olga.

"Manchester United!" – that was Danya again.

"Don't you dare!" Sergei wagged his finger at his son in mock anger. "Chelsea and nothing else!"

The Sablins were smiling again, as if by some miracle they had suddenly forgotten all their grievances. And indeed, a bit of a miracle was taking place in front of their eyes as they spoke, only they were not supposed to notice it.

The Sablins were unable to see how – behind their backs – three Horsemen, red, white and black, all dressed in medieval armour, materialised briefly and noiselessly and then melted away. It was that rare occasion when all three of them were riding together – summoned by Baba Yaga to carry out an important mission. Before joining the Sablins in the playground, she instructed her faithful knights to guard and patrol her adopted family (without revealing their presence, of course), to circle around the Sablins neck to neck, as if all three of them were part of the same Troika carriage harness, for several months in a row. With Day, Night and Sun riding next to each other as a team, time inside the circle would speed up and shrink to the point at which days followed nights and *vice versa* within moments, and that in turn would lead to the formation of a time whirlpool, into which everyone and everything within the circle would be sucked. As a result, for those inside the circle formed by the three riders, something that would normally take days would be over immediately – before you can say "knife" – whereas life outside would remain unaffected. Unlike slowing down time within the one-*versta* radius, which Yadwiga was able to do often and without much effort, shrinking time required a much more cumbersome and complicated act of magic. She could only carry it out once in a hundred years. And only in the immediate aftermath of her annual *yagishnas* split. Yadwiga was now five years short of a hundred years since using this spell for the last time – to help a male friend escape from the Lisper's Slavonia dressed in woman's garments – and therefore she was not quite sure if it was going to work. But luckily for the Sablins, it did. Whoever was measuring time gaps between magic spells and rationing them accordingly was obviously not overly bureaucratic and decided to waive the remaining five years of the taboo.

And so the Sablins did not really notice their three-month-long stay at an out-of-town *dacha* (which they had forgotten they had rented) while Yadwiga was arranging all necessary visas, invites and permissions. Just like when they were already at the airport, the Sablins did not register an unpleasant confrontation with Slavonia's customs officers who got suspicious of Yadwiga's large – much too large and heavy – chest, and were also reluctant to let through Yadwiga's cat, despite the presence of all required quarantine and injections certificates which the Cat himself brandished in front of them. To be honest, the Sablins had no idea Yadwiga had a cat in the first place – and that didn't stop them from forgetting about him all over again the moment they boarded their London-bound flight and the capacious wooden cage with the sad-looking cat inside was placed in the hold.

And of course the Sablins were unable to see three differently coloured knights astride their horses on the tarmac, under the wing of their plane, where they could not be spotted by either the passengers or the crew. They rode slowly next to each other along the airfield perimeter until the plane, having revved up its engines, started rolling ahead towards the runway, at which point they separated and galloped away in three different directions."

Chapter Seven

In which Danya gets a ride inside the mortar and his parents get lost on the Tube five years on

BULGAKOV closed the book and looked up at Yadwiga and Danya who were both shocked by what they had just heard and couldn't utter a word.

"Come on, Danya, you are welcome to ask me questions," said the Cat. "Unlike Yadwiga, I am not going to get any older than I am already. I like nothing better than a conversation, but since Yadwiga moved out of Yesterdayland, I have no-one to talk to. Snake Horinich doesn't count: he is uncouth and dumb – he can't even do a simple astral projection!"

"Shut up, Bulgakov, and stop moaning!" interrupted Yadwiga. "From what you've just read, it looks like your near future – as well as ours – will be full of excitement. But we've still got five years to wait for it and in the meantime have to face the present, or in your case, the past, meaning Yesterday. I only have one hour left here, just enough for a quick ride in my mortar unless Danya has changed his mind…"

"No, Granny, I haven't! I haven't!"

Yadwiga took Danya's hand and led him out of the Hut towards a patch of wood behind the stables. The moment they stepped off the porch, the Hut began turning back towards the forest. Danya thought he could hear it *cluck-clucking* gently as it was doing so. As they were walking across the courtyard, lit up by the skulls' glowing eyes, they could see through the open door of the stables that the black stallion

– his skin gleaming with sweat – was already back in his stall munching oats from the trough and that the adjoining cubicle, where the white horse used to stand, was empty.

"My White Knight is now out on patrol, so it will start getting light soon," said Yadwiga.

Under a branchy willow, they found a hillock covered with tarpaulin. Yadwiga lifted the cover to reveal a large iron mortar which looked like a giant elongated cocktail-mixing glass. Inside there was a pestle the size of a walking stick, and a broom.

Danya opened his mouth, but Yadwiga covered it gently with her palm.

"You want to ask what the broom is for... Well, unlike most Western witches who use it for flying, I only carry it as a precaution," she explained. "If someone starts chasing me, or if for any other reason I don't feel like being seen from the ground, I use the broom to sweep away any traces that I can leave in the sky. Doing this makes me all but invisible – the best camouflage one can think of."

Danya watched in wonder as, at the sight of their mistress, the mortar, the pestle and the broom lifted themselves off the ground and were dancing in the air as if inviting both riders to get inside and get ready for a flight.

"They don't have a lot of exercise these days," explained Yadwiga as she was helping Danya climb inside the mortar. "And they do need it, just like dogs need to be walked regularly. Otherwise, they get lazy and gradually lose their flying skills."

She climbed in after the boy and, holding the pestle with both hands, gave out a sharp, ear-piercing whistle that made Danya lose his hearing for a fraction of a second. The mortar, with Yadwiga and Danya in it, jumped up in the air and, having climbed up above the trees, froze. For a minute or so, it hung in mid-air, as if uncertain as to what to do next. When Danya thought they were about to collapse onto the ground deep down below, Yadwiga – still grabbing the pestle with both hands – leant out of the mortar up to her waist and started quickly, almost frantically, moving the pestle back and forth, as if it was the paddle of a canoe.

For a couple of seconds, the mortar remained motionless, and then – having stabilised itself in the air – began moving up and ahead, at first slowly, then faster and faster until the wind whistled in Danya's ears as loudly as his Granny's whistle before take-off.

Yadwiga's torso was well outside the mortar as she kept "rowing" ahead with the pestle.

"Don't be afraid, look down!" she shouted.

Danya stood on tiptoes and peeped out over the mortar's rim. At first, he couldn't discern much down below, apart from the dark and shapeless mass of the forest. Yet within less than a minute, the woodland ended and gave way to what looked like a real-life toy town. From above, Danya could see streets lined with minuscule lanterns, none of which were alight, and rows of miniature houses each the size of a sugar lump. Their windows were dark, with not a single glitter of light anywhere. He suddenly realised it was the town where he and his parents lived, only from above it appeared much, much smaller than it was in reality – almost like a model town he once saw in a museum. It did look more like a dummy than a real town where people (even mini-people) lived, for nothing – absolutely nothing and no-one – was moving in it, neither cars, nor trams, nor pedestrians.

"Don't be put off by the lack of life down below," shouted Yadwiga as if having read Danya's thoughts (which she had!) "Don't forget we are in Yesterdayland, whereas all the people in town, including your parents and your sister, are already in Today – that is why we cannot see them."

The sky above them was getting lighter by the minute.

"We have to go back now!" screamed Yadwiga while pushing the pestle forward, as if back-watering in the air.

The mortar made a sharp 180-degree turn in the sky, and soon they were again flying above the forest. The trees were creaking and groaning underneath and, having peeped out of the mortar for the last time, Danya got a glimpse of the miniature White Knight astride a tiny snow-white horse trotting hastily across one of the clearings.

* * *

Yadwiga opened her eyes. And so did Melissa. They were still inside the Runes bookshop in Bloomsbury. The early-eighteenth-century Queen Anne clock in the corner showed that the slowed-down spell was over and so was Yadwiga's real-time, if totally non-chronological, three-dimensional story. The cobwebs and the candelabra have disappeared, and spiral-shaped – as if bent and tied into knots – energy-saving light bulbs were filling the room with their murky, treacherous glow.

At that very moment, some early-morning pedestrians were able to spot Yadwiga's White Knight on the streets of Bloomsbury. He was dressed all in white, the horse he rode was milk-white and its harness was white. He crossed Russell Square, rode past the ornate bulk of the Russell Hotel, and then suddenly disappeared as if he had sunk into the ground. The sky above Bloomsbury started getting lighter, and soon crowds of commuters were pouring out of the Tube station, spreading rapidly in all directions.

"Good Gardner, Yadwiga, what a lot you have had to live through!" Melissa uttered after a pause.

"I certainly have," sighed her sister. "But I tell you what: I wouldn't be able to cope with it all had it not been for the family and Danya, the little boy, in particular. At times, I do feel like I am his real Granny."

"Come off it, Yadwiga! You are too young to be a Granny – just a little over a thousand years old. You are even younger than I am, if only by ten seconds or so, since I was the first to climb out of the cauldron at our birth – you and Lucinda followed!"

"This may be so, but you do not age at all, Melissa, you know that. And look at me: I do have the appearance of an old hag and will probably die fairly soon. If I keep getting older at the same rate as I have recently, I won't last for more than two or three hundred years – all thanks to Koshchei, may Perun strike him down with lightning!"

"You won't die, Yadwiga, don't you worry," said Melissa. "All we have to do is find the egg with Koshchei's life in it, and soon: three hundred years is not that long compared to eternity. But you know what: we are going to succeed!"

"You sound so sure…"

"Yes, Yadwiga, I do! Because Lucinda told me so, and she can see the future!"

"Lucinda? You saw Lucinda?" For a moment, Yadwiga seemed to forget her Koshchei-imposed taboo – and Melissa could see how two new furrow-like wrinkles cut through her forehead.

"Be careful, sister!" she screamed. "Watch what you are saying! Otherwise you won't last even three hundred years… Yes, I did see Lucinda very recently, about fifty years ago – no more. Bumped into her accidentally in Crouch End."

"I've heard about Crouch End." Yadwiga was now careful not to sound even vaguely interrogative. "In one of the books Bulgakov read to me a while ago, it was the area of London people went after dying. I even remember the name of the writer – Will Self."

"Lucinda is of course immortal, like you and me, so don't you worry," Melissa reassured her sister hastily. "She looked and behaved very much alive too – shot off before I had a chance to ask for her phone number and address! She's always been quick… I didn't even have time to find out if she was actually living there or was just visiting, and have no idea where she is now."

"I'll have to go to Crouch End and check it out," said Yadwiga. "The more so as we have actually settled not far from there. You must come over for a meal one day and meet the Sablins. You could then recharge your batteries too: they've got a nice old AER next door… But now I'd better be flying: have to find a spot for a Yesterdayland portal somewhere in London to be able to access my Hut. Also, the Sablins are in the house on their own, and I am a bit worried. They are like children – so naïve. And not a word of English among the four of them!"

"That's no good," Melissa noted gravely. "One cannot survive here without the language. You must do something about it, Yadwiga, and soon."

"And so I will, don't you worry. I've got a plan, and mark my words, by early next week they will all be as fluent in English as you and I!"

"Well, good luck to you. And in the meantime, here's something that may help you worry a bit less about your adopted family."

From a nearby chair, Melissa picked up her bulging handbag, rummaged through its contents, some of which (a lipstick, a feather, a small bell, a stack of tarot cards and a folded copy of "Pagan Dawn" magazine) spilled over onto the floor, and eventually produced a small round object, wrapped in foil.

"Here's a very recent gadget – a liquid-crystal tracking ball, with digital screen. When worried about your loved ones, simply unwrap it, rub it against your skin and say "CHO-O-OS!" The device will immediately come to life, and the screen will show what the people you are worried about are doing at that particular moment. The ball reads your heart and brain impulses and tunes automatically to those you love and are thinking of."

"Thank you, sister," said Yadwiga, accepting the ball. "This must be an expensive toy to have."

"Don't mention it! You need it more than I do, for I am completely alone and don't have anyone to miss or to worry about. Except for you and Lucinda of course, but the ball, alas, doesn't track us ved'mas, only people. Consider it a combined birthday gift for all those five hundred odd ones that I have missed – and we have a joint birthday with you of course! Now go and fly carefully: London skies are full of low-flying planes and choppers with boy-racer pilots… So good to have you around, Yadzia!"

Yadwiga was very touched by being called "Yadzia," a diminutive of Yadwiga which her sisters used to call her in their distant Krivichi past. But hundreds of years of life in the forest taught her not to succumb to emotions. She gave Melissa a quick hug, picked up the plastic bag with her flying utensils and left the shop without looking back.

* * *

"Let go of the doors please. Next stop is High Barnet!" a crackling driver's voice announced through the intercom.

Sergei was able to grasp just two words – "High Barnet" – and that was only because he did some preparatory work at home, or rather at the Woodville Avenue house, where they were put up by Yadwiga, by trying to familiarise himself with the confusing map of the London Tube, with its intertwining coloured lines standing out on the white background. He knew they were now on the black line, but had no idea it was called "Northern". At least, he was well aware of two things: the name of the station they were going to not far from which, to believe his painfully slow Internet search (in Slavonian) on Pani Czerniowiecka's ancient Amstrad computer, a job centre was located, and the direction: northward.

Irina, it has to be said, was slightly more proficient in English than her husband – to the extent that in the driver's announcement she could also recognise the word "doors" – from one of Olga's pop music tapes – although she wasn't quite sure what it actually meant.

From the simple map above the carriage door it was clear that the mysterious "High Barnet" marked the end of the black line, and they would have to get off there and change.

"Can't understand how we could have missed our station," Sergei whispered to Irina in Slavonian. For some reason, speaking a foreign language out loud didn't feel right on the London Tube. For him, at least, it didn't.

"Let us look at the map again," suggested Irina wisely, for what else could they possibly do?

They stared at the map for some more time trying to form alien-looking Latin letters into no-less-alien-sounding place names, and suddenly Irina saw what their problem was.

"Look here, Sergei! Can't you see that the black line splits into two different stretches at this station?" She pointed her finger at Camden Town. "We are on the right-hand stretch now, and the station we needed is on the opposite end of the fork!"

"This is crazy, Ira! Even the USELES Metro was easier to navigate, it seems. It's as if someone had picked up the whole of the black line and deliberately vandalised it by bending it in the middle – like Slavonian street urchins sometimes do to screen wipers of parked cars!"

"Stop complaining, Sergei. You should be grateful to this country for harbouring us and try to adjust to its ways, even if they seem strange to you."

"You are right, as always," Sergei mumbled as the train was crawling into High Barnet Station.

Having walked across the platform, the Sablins soon boarded another train in the opposite direction – towards Camden Town.

They didn't go very far on that train.

Between High Barnet and Totteridge & Whetstone, a team of ticket inspectors entered the carriage. It was one of the rare yet severe checks – part of the campaign to reduce the growing number of stowaways and fare-dodgers on the London Underground. A fat rosy-cheeked inspector did not like the look of Sergei and Irina's tickets. No wonder: the station from where they travelled and the station of their destination were both in the same zone – four – so the Sablins bought their one-zone tickets accordingly, not knowing that their unexpected detour would take them as far as Zone Six, where they were now.

"Your tickets are not valid for Zone Six, folks!" the ruddy-faced inspector informed them, cheerfully waving the pink pieces of cardboard in their faces, and added: "I am going to charge you the on-the-spot penalty fare, I am afraid!"

"No, no, no!!!" Sergei and Irina were shaking their heads emphatically, having grasped from the inspector's gestures and from his gravely sarcastic tone that their tickets were not good enough. They wanted to explain that they didn't even leave the station at High Barnet, where they ended up by mistake; that they had no idea of the black line's mysterious twists and splits; that this was their first ever London Underground ride; and that they had absolutely no cash on them. But how could they explain it all with just "yes" and "no"?

As for the inspector, he took their "no's literally – as repeated refusals to pay the fine.

"Well, in that case," he said, "we'll have to get off at the next stop and visit the nearest police station. You are grown up enough to know that fare avoidance is an offence!"

He spoke briefly into his walkie-talkie and was almost immediately joined by two more inspectors: a man and a woman. When the train came to a stop, they took Sergei and Irina by the elbows and gently pushed them towards the door and onto the platform.

And again all the Sablins' attempts to explain that they simply could not be delayed, because their two children were waiting for them at home, were futile. Their first ever journey in the UK turned out a total disaster.

* * *

Sergei and Irina would have been very surprised to learn that behind it all was no-one else but Koshchei the Deathless himself, who had decided not to let Yadwiga get away from him lightly. Shortly after the Sablins' departure from Slavonia, he came to the UK under the guise of Citizen Koshkin, the oligarch who had so brazenly taken over the Sablins' apartment, under the pretext of buying some London properties and, with luck, a couple of newspapers and football clubs too. He found out that the Sablins were going on a Tube journey the following morning, gained access to the Northern Line at three o'clock at night, when no trains were running, and, having applied his incredible strength, split its northbound stretch into two bits – the Edgware and the High Barnet branches. He then bent each of them with his bare hands – indeed like a street urchin vandalises a screen wiper on a parked car –by tying them into a knot. He did the same to the southbound stretch – just for symmetry.

"Wait a moment" you might say here. "The Northern Line was always like that – doubling in both directions at Camden Town!" But you would be wrong. The line started in the late nineteenth century as two separate railroads: the Charing Cross, Euston and Hampstead Railway in the north and the City and South London Railway in the south, joined together at Euston. Indeed, since approximately 1900, we remember the Northern Line more or less as it is now – with its two northbound branches which initially ended at Highgate and Golders Green respectively and were later extended. The key word here is "remember," for after splitting up the line to confuse the Sablins and to add to Yadwiga's troubles, Koshchei made sure there remained neither the vaguest recollection in anyone's mind nor the tiniest trace on any map of the Northern Line as it used to be – straight and uncomplicated. To divert attention from his horrible actions and to distract Londoners from questioning the bizarre shape of the Northern Line too often, he made sure that the trains on it were always packed full, uncomfortable and slow. He introduced such enigmatic concepts as "signal problems", "leaves slippage" and "power failure", the exact meaning of which nobody could quite understand, but which were nevertheless useful when trying to justify why the Northern Line so often malfunctioned. For Koshchei, the world's most powerful magician, achieving all of this was as simple and as quick as swiping an Oyster card on entering a Tube station for an average London commuter.

Chapter Eight

In which Danya and Olga explore their first English garden while Yadwiga and their parents have their first encounter with the police

I WONDER what happened to Mum and Dad?" Olga said to noone in particular, her eyes fixed on the flashing TV screen where one of the previous season's QI shows was being replayed. Olga could not understand a single word of the show, but still watched it because she found one of the contestants, a youngish middle-aged fellow with long curly hair who never seemed to come up with a correct answer, cute.

"Didn't you hear them saying they were going for a walk?" Danya replied from behind his old USELES-made gaming console.

"Some walk! They've been away for four hours already and I am getting hungry," his sister retorted. "Could have at least given us a ring to say they were being delayed!"

"A ring from what? They haven't had a chance to get mobiles yet. And haven't they left some food for us in the fridge?" asked Danya.

"Not a thing! That fridge is empty as a stretch of tundra in winter!" Olga pouted her lips.

"I am starving too," said Danya with a sigh. "Maybe Granny will come back soon and bring some food?"

"I doubt it," shrugged Olga. "She is probably still with her sister. Said she would stay overnight and would see some friends this morning. How come she has friends and relatives here when she's so old – and we don't?"

"Our Granny has friends everywhere, and she is not old!" Danya retorted.

He came up to the bay window overlooking a vast rectangular back garden, with several bare fruit trees and stalks of pampas grass sticking out at the edges. At the very bottom of the garden there was a swing.

"I think I can see some pears left on a tree at the far end," he said.

"Pears in winter? You must be dreaming!" his sister snapped.

"You think you know everything, Olga. But I read somewhere that winter in England is often mild and some fruit's seasons run well into it. Why don't you unglue yourself from that stupid telly and see for yourself?"

Reluctantly, Olga got off the sofa and joined her brother.

"You are right, Danya. They do look like pears. I normally don't eat fruit, but I'm so ravenous that I wouldn't mind a bite or two now."

"Neither would I. But Mum and Dad have strictly forbidden us to leave the flat, and we promised them we wouldn't."

"Well, firstly, we are only going into the garden which is part of the flat... well, almost... Secondly, they are not very good at sticking to their own promise to return home soon, so why should we stick to ours?"

Remembering his disastrous early childhood attempt at reaching a nice-looking waxen apple under the ceiling, Danya was still apprehensive. But he could also see that Olga had a point. Besides, he was very hungry.

"OK, let's put on our coats and pop out for a minute," he decided. He could almost feel the bitter-sweet taste of those small and wrinkled pears in his mouth.

* * *

On the way home, Yadwiga decided to check out a couple of possible places for a new Yesterdayland portal. It was a matter of some urgency, for the empty Elm Tree Wood cottage, inside which she had temporarily hidden her Hut on chicken's legs, with Bulgakov in it, had just been bought and taken off the market. New owners were about to move in, so the Hut had to be relocated to a new hiding place ASAP. And despite Bulgakov's protestations, there couldn't be a better way of hiding it than in Yesterday, where only stray *ved'mas* or some drunk wood goblins could stumble upon it by accident. But even they would normally mistake it for a quirky hunting lodge left behind in Yesterdayland by some demoted USELES functionaries, still hoping for the return of the old Equalist times.

Yadwiga had a list of possible locations put together by her friend Pani Czerniowiecka, who had lived in London for most of her life and knew it well. Pani Chirnowecka, or Ms Black, was in fact a *dzivozoana*, or a *mamuna* – a peculiar creature originating from the swamps of Eastern Poland; a woman who was never quite alive, or never quite dead, and whose existence alternated between the house in Woodville Avenue and a spacious sarcophagus in the nearby Highgate Cemetery. This quality made her an ideal absentee landlady, during her cemetery periods that is, the latest of which had just begun.

The first on the list was the property at 23-24, Leinster Gardens in Bayswater. It was daytime, so Yadwiga was careful not to fly too low. Having made two circles above Paddington Green, she landed in an empty back garden, concealed the mortar and the pestle under a pile of fallen leaves and limped out into the street for a closer look.

She was not immediately able to spot a row of Georgian terrace windows which at first glance appeared heavily curtained, but on closer inspection could be recognised for what they were – a hoax and a *trompe l'oeil*. From the brief description Pani Czerniowiecka had kindly attached to each structure on her list prior to retiring to her cosy sarcophagus for a year or so, Yadwiga learned that the windows had been masterfully drawn onto the yellow stuccoed facade of the house to conceal a stretch of the 1860s Metropolitan Railway extension planned to run straight through the Leinster Gardens terrace, so that the houses at numbers 23 and 24 had to be demolished. The dwellers in the nearby buildings, however, did not like the prospect of living in a mutilated road and demanded that the frontages of the ruined houses, including part of a balcony with flowers, be retained, even if by deceit. It was a classic case of window-dressing, very familiar to Yadwiga, which was often used in old Slavonia and in the USELES to mislead the tsars and other powers-that-be by hiding abominable poverty and dirt behind nice-looking facades of prosperity, hastily constructed on cheerfully painted pieces of cardboard or such like.

But for her current purpose of hiding a portal to Yesterdayland the spot seemed ideal, for there was nothing behind the painted windows, and even the passengers of the District and Circle Line Tube trains running underneath the paintings were not supposed to notice the fake.

Having made up her mind, Yadwiga was about to retrace her steps towards Bayswater Road when she was approached by a neatly dressed young man with a piece of paper in his hand.

"Excuse me, Ma'am, do you live in this house?" he asked Yadwiga, pointing at number 23.

"Even if I did, I wouldn't have to tell you, son, for it is frankly none of your business," Yadwiga retorted curtly, having realised she had just gained another wrinkle – in addition to the two she had acquired earlier that morning due to a momentary loss of control inside Melissa's shop.

"Yes, except that I am with the police." The young man produced an ID badge from his pocket and brandished it in Yadwiga's face.

"It doesn't matter if you are the police or whatever. Had you been the Metropolitan Police Commissioner himself, you'd still have to officially arrest me first before interrogating!" Yadwiga turned her back to the young man and started shuffling away from him.

"Ma'am, please wait a moment," the young man pleaded to Yadwiga's receding back. "It is not an interrogation, but just one quick question: do you know the people living in number 23-24 and, if yes, have you noticed anything suspicious in their behaviour of late?"

Yadwiga stopped and was about to tell this overly persistent youngster off properly – in her impeccable Cockney – but was distracted by a loud man's laughter coming from behind her back. Even before she had time to turn, she knew it was not her pushy young interlocutor who was laughing. Two much older men were striding hastily towards them from across the road. They were both wearing civilians suits and ties, yet their upright and confident – as if commanding – posture gave a clue to their true occupation.

"Easy, Thompson," one of the men said to the youngster before turning to Yadwiga. "And please accept our sincere apologies, Ma'am!"

"We owe you an explanation," the other man chuckled. "We are CID officers from Paddington Green Police Station round the corner. It's been an age-long tradition with our unit to send new recruits or probationers, as we call them, to this house, in which, as we all know, nobody lives because it is a fake, to conduct enquiries as a baptism or initiation of sorts. And while an aspiring police constable, like Thompson here, is making a fool of himself, we senior officers watch him from round the corner and laugh… So please do forgive us for the disturbance."

"Never mind, officer," Yadwiga tried not to sound too relieved. "It is a nice old tradition, as I can see. Even if a bit childish!"

With this, she walked away from the three policemen, or, to be more exact, from the two facetious policemen and one puzzled police trainee. Only this time she headed in the direction opposite to her flying kit's hiding place. She thought she'd walk around the block first. Just to be on the safe side. And so she did feel grateful for the unexpected intrusion which made it absolutely clear that the fake Leinster Gardens terrace was unsuitable for the Yesterdayland portal: she didn't want policemen or – worse – aspiring policemen prying inside the place every day.

In short, she had to keep looking.

* * *

As Yadwiga was circling the streets of Bayswater, at the other end of London, namely in Barnet, Sergei and Irina were having a much less pleasant police encounter inside Totteridge Police Station, into which they were frogmarched by a team of overzealous ticket inspectors. They were promptly put in front of a duty officer – a young police sergeant, tired after a night shift and eager to get home. He was visibly irritated by these new detainees who meant more work and possibly overtime too.

"These two are fare-dodgers, sergeant," puffed out the ticket inspector. "Refused to pay the correct fare."

He paused and added: "They don't speak a word of English, or pretend not to."

"If so, how did you grasp their refusal to pay the fare?" the duty officer enquired logically.

"They kept shaking their heads frantically, which to me means 'no,'" shrugged the ticket inspector.

"Not if they were from Greece, or, say, from Bulgaria, where shaking one's head means 'yes' and nodding 'no,'" the knowledgeable sergeant replied and looked at the foreign couple who by then had all but given up attempts to explain themselves with gestures and were just sitting in front of him quietly and staring at the floor. To the duty officer's experienced eye, these two did not look like criminals – just two confused and tired individuals, very much like himself at the end of the shift.

"*Parlez-vous Anglais?*" he asked them. No effect whatsoever. He then repeated the same question in several other European languages, and completely exhausted his knowledge of obscure tongues which included Estonian (he had had to deal with a dangerously fast driver from that small Baltic country the other day):

"*Kas te oskate vene inglise?*"

The latter didn't fail to impress the waiting ticket inspector, who now realised that the stowaways were in proper hands and left the station, but it failed to provoke any reaction from the detainees.

The duty officer pressed a button on the desk panel in front of him and lifted the in-built receiver.

"Operator, can we summon Mr Kashin for some urgent interpreting please?" he said.

"Sure we can, serge!" was the reply. "Which language?"

"How would I know? Something East European, I would guess. But doesn't Kashin claim to have about fifty languages at his fingertips? I'm sure it will be one of those."

"Yes, he is a real treasure, Mr Kashin; he has helped us out many times! What would we do without him when most of the offenders in London are foreign?"

"Enough said, operator. Just call him immediately," the duty officer replaced the receiver. He didn't quite like the operator's politically incorrect mode of thinking.

"I am sorry, folks, but we don't have a waiting room in this station. The lady can sit in my office, but the gentleman here, I am afraid, will have to go to a detention cell until the interpreter arrives," he said to the visibly distraught Sergei and Irina without any hope of being understood – just for the sake of it. "We have good company for you there today, young man. I only hope you like football…"

* * *

With an effort, Danya opened the balcony door leading to the garden. Its hinges were stiff and rusty – clearly it hadn't been used very often by Pani Czerniowiecka, the house owner (*mamunas*, alias *dziwozonas*, do not need much fresh air, even when alive).

"It's freezing," complained Olga. She hadn't bothered to put on her coat and was shivering.

"We won't be long. Just quickly pick up some pears and get back inside," reassured Danya.

To get to the opposite end of the garden, they had to cross a large neglected lawn the size of basketball pitch. Overgrown with the previous year's grass, it was damp and muddy. The children walked slowly in their flimsy slippers trying not to get their feet wet. They were about half way to their goal and could already clearly see several appetising pears in a tree next to the rusty see-saw, when their attention got diverted by a loud wheezing, buzzing sound coming from behind the fence separating Pani Czerniowiecka's garden from the plot of the house next door. It was similar to the noise of a disturbed giant bumblebee or to that of a vacuum cleaner when you press the start button accidentally. They looked in the direction of the sound and froze: a dark silhouette of a woman rose from behind the fence. She was sitting astride a gleaming round object (or was it a creature?) and clutching a hose (or was it the creature's trunk?) in her hands as if steering or just trying to keep her balance. It took the bizarre flying object just a couple of seconds to lift itself high above the garden and vanish into the clouds.

"Did you see it too, Olya?" Danya screamed to his sister. "Because if you didn't, I must be going crazy!"

"Don't you worry, Dan'ka: you are no more and no less crazy than you were a minute ago!" Olga yelled back. "I also saw the old hag riding a vacuum cleaner. And she looked as real as you and me, unless we are both hallucinating from hunger!"

"She must have taken off from the back garden next to ours," muttered Danya. He immediately thought of Granny Yadwiga, of course, but the sphere the woman appeared to be flying did not look at all like a mortar. Whatever it was and whoever the flying woman could be, it was best to keep Olga out of it, he decided. The existence of Baba Yaga and other *ved'mas* was his and Granny Yadwiga's big secret, and he would do anything to keep it as such.

"You know what, Olya, I think I have a fever," he said suddenly and put his hand on his forehead. "I can see black circles dancing in front of my eyes. And that flying woman was probably indeed just an illusion..."

"What are you talking about? I saw her too!" Olga was getting angry.

"Are you sure, sister? Are you absolutely sure? You could be just feeling dizzy with hunger!"

"What do you mean?"

"I mean that there are things in life that are best forgotten, as if they never happened. For your own good…"

"Are you trying to teach me how to live, you squab? I am your older sister, don't forget!" Olga was now fuming with rage.

"Older but not necessarily cleverer!"

In the heat of the argument, they failed to notice a large black cat in the far corner of the garden. Had Danya seen him, he'd immediately recognise his learned friend Bulgakov. But he didn't.

"What a mess," the Cat mumbled to himself. "Yadwiga must have forgotten to activate the astral firewall separating Today and Yesterday. Otherwise, I wouldn't be able to see the kids now… Wait a moment: if I can see them, it means that they can see me too. And not just me but also the Astral Energy Receiver customers at number 127. They could have even seen Dion taking off a minute ago! I am not worried about Danya, because he knows, but his sister… She could be trouble! I knew something was not right when I saw their parents walking past the Hut this morning. What a horrible oversight by Yadwiga! She must be getting old indeed!"

Bulgakov hid behind a bush and kept thinking aloud – a habit resulting from years of loneliness and the lack of interlocutors in Yesterdayland.

"Well, I haven't done magic for a while, but will have to now, it seems. The children must be made to forget whatever they might have seen. Otherwise, we'd be facing a serious breach of time and space parameters here. A very serious breach!"

He gave out a prolonged, yet hardly audible, hiss, jumped up in the air and vanished…

"Sorry, what were you saying?" Danya asked his sister.

"Nothing much. Just that I am hungry and freezing. Let's pick up the wretched pears and get back inside!"

And so they did.

Chapter Nine

In which Sergei confronts football hooligans and Yadwiga loses her flying kit

H EY, where are you from? Ah? He must be blooming deaf, this gypsy bloke, innit?"

Sergei looked up. A porky, unshaven character was staring at him with malice from the opposite bench.

"Nah, Bonehead, he is not deaf – just a bloody foreigner. One of those who come here to steal our jobs, houses and girls!"

The last tirade stemmed from another stubbly type sitting next to Bonehead. He was wearing a rumpled, dirty T-Shirt with "Go, Sandham, Go!" written on it. And although Sergei could not understand a single word of what his cellmates were saying, from the tone of their voices and from their facial expressions it was obvious that they were neither enquiring about his health nor wishing him a nice day. They looked aggressive and, for all he knew, were probably verbally abusing him.

"I am with you, Sammy," – that was the third man speaking. Unlike Sammy and Bonehead, who were both tall and corpulent, this one was thin, short and feeble. "I bet he doesn't even know what 'football' means."

"I bet you he does, Pete!" said Sammy. "On top of our girls and our jobs, they've nicked this great English game from us too and are now trying to beat us at it, these foreign cheeks. Even our Sandham Warriors have a Polish goalkeeper! And I tell you what: until we get rid of that blooming Pole, we'll never qualify for League One and every flipping little team will be beating us, like those bloody Barnet Bees yesterday… Poles are OK as goal posts, not as goalkeepers!"

He cackled at his own pun.

"Shush, Sammy," Bonehead interrupted. "Cops may hear you swearing and keep us here for another night…"

"They have no right! We shouldn't be here at all, if you ask me. What have we done? Just had a couple of pints at the Queen's Head on the way from the blasted Underhill Stadium and were defending ourselves against some drunk Barnet supporters. OK, we were pretty plastered ourselves, but for a good reason: it is not often that your team loses one to eight! At football – not at flipping cricket!"

Sergei recognised the word "football" again, nodded and smiled, hoping to mollify his cell neighbours. It was a mistake.

"Look at the foreigner. He is laughing at us!" said Pete, whose full nickname was actually Parasol Pete, for, unlike his macho soccer hooligan mates, he was a bit of a wimp, didn't like rain and always brought an old twisted umbrella to the stadium.

"He sure does!" echoed Sammy, whose own nickname was Steaming Sammy – owing to his irritability and short temper, which was legendary among Sandham Warriors fans.

"Let's rub that nasty gypsy grin off his ugly face then!" commanded Bonehead.

All three of them stood up and closed in on Sergei, who, apart from being soft and kind, was a Master of Sports in Salambo – a traditional Slavonian type of wrestling combining elements of self-defence, boxing and martial arts. He had learned it at university and was even once the country's runner-up in the middleweight category. Far from pugnacious, the only real-life fights Sergei had had a chance to be involved in so far were verbal battles with Irina. It was clear that now was the time to use his wrestling skills for self-defence.

As Bonehead's bony fist flew towards his face, Sergei blocked the punch with his left elbow and simultaneously twisted Bonehead's wrist with his right hand. Bonehead squealed with pain and collapsed on the cold cement floor of the cell. Then, Sergei quickly tripped

Sammy, who dashed at him just like a puffing steam engine and, having caught Pete's thin neck in an arm lock, threw him over his back in a classic and seemingly effortless shoulder roll. Parasol Pete hit the floor with a thud – like a sack of potatoes dropped by a careless stevedore.

"What's going on here?" The duty sergeant was entering the cell. Behind him stood a tall thin man with an old-fashioned pincenez on his nose which gave him a somewhat owlish look. It was Mr Kashin, the interpreter.

* * *

Yadwiga was in a hurry. She kept worrying about the Sablins, and her instinct was to abandon the search for a Yesterdayland portal and fly back home. On the other hand, she realised the urgency of finding one as soon as she could: keeping her Hut, with Bulgakov in it, inside the Elm Tree Wood Cottage was getting more and more dangerous. The new owners were due to turn up any moment, and contrary to what Bulgakov thought, she had not forgotten to erect the time firewall between Today and Yesterday; she hadn't even tried to do it, for how can one separate these two major time dimensions without a portal? On top of it all, Snake Horinich had suddenly turned up on their Woodville Avenue doorstep the previous morning: he allegedly got bored in Yesterdayland, with only the pair of hands and his own heads for company. With no wall between the two time dimensions, he simply flew from one to the other. Luckily, it happened at four o'clock in the morning when all the Sablins were asleep. Yadwiga had somehow managed to persuade Snake Horinich to stay put until she reinstalled the wall, hiding two of his heads under his wings and temporarily replacing the single-headed red dragon on the roof of the house at number 125. Bored by years of sitting on top of the roof, the latter was more than happy to do the swap and to stretch his wings, which had gone stiff with inactivity... Thankfully, despite his ferocious looks, Snake Horinich was an obedient and patient creature: he agreed to keep quiet for a day or so and was so far doing fine. He stayed motionless on the roof and had so much grown into his decorative role that neither pedestrians in Woodville Avenue, nor even their dogs – let alone the Sablins – had been able to spot the change.

"I must find the beast a home soon – a hangar or a disused garage," thought Yadwiga while steering her mortar through thick rain clouds in London's permanently overcast winter sky.

She had only one possible portal site left to look at – Ely Place.

After her unexpected encounter with the three policemen in Leinster Gardens, Yadwiga had inspected and discarded three more locations from Pani Czerniowiecka's list: the Kingsway Tram Subway had been out of use since 1957 and would have been ideal, had it not become home to a particularly noisy restaurant and a venue for occasional art shows too – no privacy whatsoever! The nearby abandoned Aldwich Tube station would have been another great location for the portal, had it not been used much too often as a film set. As for the house at 59 ½, Southwark Street, which aroused Pani Czerniowiecka's and Yadwiga's interest due to the promising "1/2" in its number (the portal could have been easily hidden in the missing second half!), it was totally out of the question, for it now housed London Council's Community Services – a serious organisation often visited by people with lots of spare time on their hands and therefore with levels of curiosity much higher than average.

Having narrowly avoided a collision with the tall spire of St Bride's – a wedding-cake-shaped journalists' church in Fleet Street – Yadwiga soon reached Holborn Circus and was floating in the air above the roof of Maxwell House, former home of the Mirror Group newspapers where, as Pani Czerniowiecka had assured her, there had to be a private helipad of the late media tycoon Robert Maxwell onto which she should be able to land smoothly. To her surprise, Yadwiga realised that Maxwell House as such was no longer there. On its spot was a modern glass and concrete building, with a large sign, "Sainsbury's Store Support," at the entrance and not a trace of a helipad on its flat, glass-covered and, no doubt, slippery roof, landing onto which was precarious.

Well, due to her peculiar semi-dead existence, Pani Czerniowiecka could be forgiven for being somewhat out of touch with reality.

Having made a couple of circles above Holborn, Yadwiga saw a pretty dome-like cupola on top of the otherwise grim-looking HSBC bank building to the left of the Sainsbury's Store Support building and decided she could safely land next to it on the roof. Having packed her flying kit in the same black bin bag she always carried with her on her flights, she easily found the hatch leading to the staircase and lifts.

Yadwiga hid the bag with its contents in an empty cleaner's cubicle inside a ladies toilet on the sixth floor and took the lift down. Ely Place – the last privately owned street in London – was just a short walk away. According to Pani Czerniowiecka's written directions, however, the Holborn Circus end of it was guarded by a beadle – an employee of the Commissioners of Ely, an elected body which governed that peculiar one-street "mini-state" in the very centre of London. Very few people knew that the straight and treeless lane was not geographically part of London. It was a little corner of Cambridgeshire, still enjoying freedom from entry by the London police, except at the invitation of the Commissioners, who were elected every year.

Ely Place was simultaneously in London and NOT in London, and eighty odd miles away. Its correct address was: Ely Place, Holborn Circus, London, Cambridgeshire! It was literally neither here, nor there – a perfect place for a portal where two different time dimensions, Today and Yesterday, could be joined together with minimum effort. At least, that was what the temporarily deceased Pani Czerniowiecka had reckoned when she put Ely Place on her list.

For obvious reasons, Yadwiga chose not to walk past the beadle's cabin and gained access to Ely Place via a carefully concealed gateway off Hatton Garden. Walking through the dark narrow passageway past Ye Olde Mitre Tavern through which the border with

Cambridgeshire ran, was indeed like travelling through a natural time portal. Even before she reached the street as such, Yadwiga knew that she had found what she was looking for. And having examined Ely Place thoroughly, she decided that the best spot for the portal would be an old, dark and permanently deserted crypt inside the magnificent St Etheldreda Chapel in the middle of the street.

Mission accomplished, Yadwiga was plodding back to Holborn Circus via the same gateway when she remembered Melissa's present and decided to check on the Sablins.

She took the liquid-crystal ball out of her pocket, removed the foil and rubbed it against her wrist while whispering: "*CHOO-OS!!*"

The tiny high-definition digital screen came to life, and Yadwiga could suddenly see Sergei inside what looked like a police station being interrogated via an interpreter. "Totteridge Police Station, distance ten miles," the crystal ball announced in a dry robotic voice. The scene was disturbing, to say the least, but it was only when Yadwiga squinted at the screen to get a better view and realised WHO the interpreter actually was that she got seriously scared.

She knew there was not a second to lose, because it was she and only she who could save Sergei and the whole Sablin family from the awful disaster they were now facing.

As fast as her dignity and fragile build allowed, she ran towards the grey HSBC building, took the lift to the sixth floor and hurried towards the Ladies'. The cleaner's cubicle was empty, with no trace of the black bin bag with her mortar, pestle and broom!

Yadwiga had no time to think what might have happened to her flying kit and decided to worry about it later. Luckily, her magic ball of wool, a *ved'ma*-tested GPS of sorts, was still with her. Having taken it out of her other pocket, she placed it on the tiled toilet floor. The ball started rolling slowly, as if inviting her to follow. Yadwiga could see it was not fast enough: it would take her days to reach Totteridge if she chose to walk behind it, as she had done so many times in the past. But now she was neither in the forest of her youth, nor even in Slavonia. Yadwiga picked up the ball of wool from the floor, wound back the thread and returned it to her pocket. The situation was desperate, with only minutes to find a solution.

She left the bathroom and climbed up the steep staircase to the roof.

Standing inside the cupola, she lifted her head towards the clouds and, with her hands pointing upwards, began chanting: *"Tai Re Re Re!! Tai Re Re Re Re!!"*

It was a special emergency call for Snake Horinich, whose six super-sensitive ears were able to pick up this particular phonetic combination – *"Tai Re Re Re!! Tai Re Re Re Re!!"* – and the air oscillations it generated from many miles. Yet Yadwiga was unsure if Horinich's present state as a roof sculpture would deter him from hearing it.

"Please, please, Horinich, dear, hear me!" she was whispering, having forgotten all other mantras, spells and incantations and focusing all her spiritual energy on just this one: *"Tai Re Re Re!! Tai Re Re Re Re!! Tai Re Re Re!!"*

A strange thing was happening to the sculpture of the red "Welsh" dragon on the roof of house number 125. First, the dragon's tail moved slowly up and down, as if stretching after a long sleep, then his head started turning left and right – like that of a troubled bird. Within a couple of seconds, two more heads and necks were miraculously added to the dragon's elongated torso, who began to slowly climb down the roof until it reached the edge, at which point two vast and waving membranous wings unfolded. The creature then took off the roof and, spitting out smoke and flames from all his three mouths, flew over the street and headed south.

But the few pedestrians hurrying towards the warmth of their houses did not bother to look up that evening, and Snake Horinich's spectacular take-off, as well as the temporary gap on the spot of the roof where the red dragon "sculpture" used to be, remained unnoticed and unrecorded both from outside house number 125 and from the inside, where Danya and his sister Olga – hungry, exhausted and frustrated by their parents' and Granny's prolonged and unexplained absence – were both fast asleep on the lounge room sofa.

Chapter Ten

In which Yadwiga clashes with Koshchei and wins

W HAT'S going on here??" the duty officer shouted in amazement.

The sight was indeed compelling: three soccer hooligans sprawled on the cement floor of the cell, with Sergei, dishevelled and breathing heavily, towering above them.

"It is all his fault!" Bonehead jumped up and pointed at Sergei with his hairy nicotine-stained index finger. "This bloody foreigner wanted to kill us!"

"Yes, he did, he did!" his mates Sammy and Pete echoed while still horizontal.

"You don't seem very dead to me," the sergeant grinned. "I bet you guys poured bucketfuls of abuse onto the poor man before he had no choice but to shut you up. Now get off the floor and put yourselves in order: supper is on its way!"

He then turned to Sergei: "Sorry, mate, I don't know your name and you probably do not understand a word I am saying, but you should have called me or another constable, instead of introducing your own vigilante justice here, understood?"

Sergei smiled and shook his head.

"So I thought. That's why we've called Mr Kashin, who will help us understand each other. Let's go back to my office and have a chat, shall we?"

Behind his back, tall and stooping Mr Kashin cleared his throat and said to Sergei in perfect Slavonian:

"I am Boris Kashin, your interpreter. Come out of the cell and follow us."

"You could have said hello first," Sergei remarked quietly. "And may I ask how you've guessed that I was from Slavonia?"

"Because I used to live in Slavonia myself and know your type! And remember: it is the sergeant and I who ask questions here. You answer!"

Koshchei – and it was him of course – was annoyed with himself for the miscalculation: of course, he should have tried several other languages first, otherwise the policeman could start wondering if he had already known who Sergei was. And his fears proved justified.

"Which language did you speak to the detainee?" the duty officer asked Kashin-Koshchei as they walked along the corridor: Sergei in front, with the other two following him.

"Slavonian, sir. I thought I'd try it first. It was a lucky coincidence we got it right at the first go." Koshchei deliberately said "we," trying to ingratiate himself with the sergeant and to team up with him. His tactics worked.

"Well done, Mr Kashin," said the policeman. "With your vast experience you must be able to tell where a person is from by simply looking at them."

"You are too kind, sir."

They entered the office, where Irina was waiting, anxious and red-eyed. She ran up to Sergei and hugged him.

"When will they let us go?" she asked.

"Don't worry, Ira. It will all be fine," her husband replied. "We haven't committed any crimes and they should let us out soon. Britain is a democratic country, after all..."

"Democratic it may be, but not for scum like you!" said Kashin-Koshchei in Slavonian. Sergei dashed at him, but had to restrain himself.

"Who is this horrible man?" asked Irina.

"He is an interpreter."

"Brilliant. Why can't he help us explain to the policeman here that we have two underage children and an old lady waiting for us at home and getting hungry?"

"Not so fast, lady, not so fast," Koshchei interrupted. "Otherwise my interpretation may not turn out as correct and as precise as you would wish."

He then said in English to the sergeant: "The female detainee here expresses her anger at being kept without a warrant and threatens to write about it to the Independent Police Complaints Commission."

"Does she really? I would have never imagined they had heard of the IPCC in Slavonia. Besides, which language is she planning to write a complaint in? I doubt they have Slavonian speakers at the IPCC…"

"Don't underestimate these people, sir, if I may volunteer my humble opinion. They may not be as naïve as they appear!"

"Let's find out," the officer decided. "Can you please ask them when they arrived in the UK and what the purpose of their visit was?"

Kashin-Koshchei turned towards the Sablins and spoke in Slavonian: "The officer here wants to know what crimes you have committed while in the UK and says that if you confess all your misdeeds voluntarily, he will try and reduce your prison terms."

"What nonsense!" Sergei cried out. "We haven't committed any crimes in the UK or anywhere else. We were simply trying to find a job centre and got lost on the Underground!"

"The man says that he refuses to answer your stupid – I am sorry, sir, that was what he said – stupid questions and demands to be released immediately, so that they can resume their terrorist activities…"

"What activities? Are you sure you got it right, Mr Kashin?"

"Absolutely sure. He said terrorist activities!"

The policeman stretched out his hand to pick up the phone, but changed his mind.

"Don't translate this, but I think they are deliberately trying to implicate themselves because they have no home to go to and simply want to spend the night under a roof. This happens often. So please tell them to stop fooling around and answer my questions properly!"

Koshchei nodded.

"The police officer here says he doesn't believe a word of what you are saying and suggests for the last time that you acknowledge your horrible crimes immediately!"

"But this is blackmail!" screamed Irina. "We have nothing to acknowledge and demand to be seen by a senior officer!"

"I agree with my wife," said Sergei. "He has no right to speak to us in this manner."

"The detainees say that among other terrorist tasks they were assigned to carry out while in the UK on behalf of SIC – Slavonia's Intelligence Command, of which they are both senior members – were assassinations of Her Majesty the Queen and the Prime Minister…"

"That's enough!" The duty officer grabbed the phone and opened his mouth to ask the operator to connect him to Scotland Yard's Anti-Terrorist Unit immediately – when all of a sudden he froze in his chair, with his hand, clutching the receiver, hanging in mid-air… Sergei and Irina froze in their chairs too, and the last digit on the display of the large electronic clock on the wall opposite the duty officer's desk stopped blinking and stayed unchanged. Down the corridor, inside the detention cell, Bonehead's meaty hand holding a spoonful of soup stopped half-way to his wide-open gullet, as if suspended from an invisible thread, while Parasol Pete and Steaming Sammy were staring at him intently with their half-open mouths full of food, not moving either.

Koshchei watched in disbelief as the door of the duty officer's office was flung open and in came Yadwiga.

Before he could click his fingers to have her turned into stone, she spoke in a loud voice, hoarsened from the flight through the chill of the London night astride Snake Horinich's middle neck:

"Greetings to you, Koshchei, from Baron Edward Bulwer-Lytton!"

She was bluffing of course and taking a considerable risk on the basis of what Bulwer-Lytton himself told her during her flying (in the true sense of the word) visit to Knebworth in 1843 when he had just finished his novel *Zanoni*, largely based on the stories which Yadwiga herself shared with him. Here it has to be noted that Bulwer-Lytton had always had a soft spot for Yadwiga, with whom he had a short, but tempestuous, romance in the 1840s, after his famously dysfunctional marriage to Rosina Wheeler came to an acrimonious end. Koshchei was the prototype of the novel's anti-hero, Mejnour – a calm and "bloodless" man who achieved immortality, but was devoid of all passion or feeling. Like Koshchei, Mejnour lived in a mountain castle, masterfully described by Bulwer-Lytton from Yadwiga's own recollections: she knew the interior and the exterior of that castle, which used to be her prison, only too well… Yadwiga, or rather her fictional alter ego called Viola, for whom Mejnour experienced (for he could not *feel* in the proper sense of this word) a hopeless and unrequited affection, also featured in *Zanoni*.

As we have noted already, Bulwer-Lytton was not just a writer, but also a magician with the gift of clairvoyance and prediction. The interesting thing about *Zanoni* was that in the novel the immortal Mejnour, alias Koshchei, eventually died trying to save Viola's life, having decided that it was only through death that he could achieve true immortality. And although Bulwer-Lytton did not go into much detail about how exactly Mejnour died, he mentioned to Yadwiga that the way to his death lay through a doorway inside a bookshop in Covent Garden. That was all she knew. Her thinking was that if Koshchei was aware of the novel and of being portrayed in it, he should be taking interest in and probably be afraid of anything that was connected with Bulwer-Lytton, who could have uncovered the secret of his death and, for all Koshchei knew, could still be keeping it (if it is assumed that the writer himself possessed some form of immortality, despite his publicly proclaimed demise in 1873).

Yadwiga's calculations proved right: the name of Bulwer-Lytton was probably the only sound in the world capable of stopping Koshchei in his tracks. Yadwiga could see that he was shocked, but he tried to pretend he wasn't.

"Yadwiga, darling! So good to see you are still alive! What a pleasant surprise!" he croaked with a grimace that was supposed to pass for a smile. Smiling was another thing, apart from feeling, of which Koshchei was utterly incapable.

"Don't you 'darling' me, Koshchei," said Yadwiga. "Our 'darling' times were brief and have been over for hundreds of years. I am here to collect these two people," she pointed at Sergei and Irina — both motionless behind the duty officer's desk. "And if you try to hurt them or me again, I'll have no choice but to follow the old Baron's advice to the letter!"

Koshchei emitted a dry laugh without a smile. "You are pulling my leg again, Yadwiga. Bulwer-Lytton cannot advise you on anything any longer simply because he has been dead for a hundred and thirty years!"

"As Bulwer-Lytton himself once wrote, 'a man is ignorant in proportion to his arrogance,'" said Yadwiga. "Yes, he might have been dead, although I wouldn't vouch for it. But even if he is, we still have *Zanoni*!"

"Don't make me laugh, Yadwiga. *Zanoni* is just a book, a novel, pure fantasy…"

"I will respond to that with a quote from this very novel, Koshchei: 'If not in books, sir, where else am I to obtain information?' It is a question, but a rhetorical one which does not require an answer and therefore doesn't add another wrinkle to my face! Yes, there is *Zanoni*, but there is also another book — yet unpublished and probably even unwritten — that my friend Bulgakov recently introduced me to. My next quote comes from it, and I suspect you are not going to like it, Koshchei!"

Yadwiga closed her eyes and – in a voice that sounded cold and alien – slowly, as if trying to recall a passage she was asked to memorise, uttered the following:

"The Baron was right! And so was Lucinda! Here it is, at last!!" exclaimed Danya. "The egg with the needle inside! Koshchei's death is at the tip of this needle. If we break it – Koshchei will die!"

"Wait a second, Danya," said Yadwiga. "Please give me the egg. I want to handle it myself…"

Yadwiga opened her eyes: "That will do for the time being. Now get out of my way, Citizen Koshkin, alias interpreter Kashin, and allow us to leave the station!"

Koshchei was visibly shaken.

"What's the title of this book you've just quoted from?"

"I know you are doing it deliberately, Koshchei: showering me with questions, hoping I'll drop dead here and now! I won't. Not just yet… The book is *Granny Yaga* by Vitali Vitaliev, but that's of no use to you because it is not just one tome, and that particular volume in the series which I've quoted from hasn't been written yet. But as my sister Lucinda tells me, it will certainly come out in the future, and that is why you won't be able to stop it from being completed – now or ever!"

The mention of Lucinda was Yadwiga's second attempt at bluffing, and, like the first one, it was successful.

"We shall see about it, we shall see…" mumbled Koshchei, who appeared to have shrunk all of a sudden. He was also stooping much more than before, so much that his head was almost touching the linoleum floor and his pince-nez fell off his nose.

"You win for now, Baba Yaga," he muttered as he floated in the air a couple of metres above the floor. "But as one French military commander used to say, I may have lost the battle, but I haven't lost the war! You will hear from me soon, Yadwiga, darling. Very, very soon!"

Having said that, Koshchei arranged himself horizontally, flew slowly towards the station door, which opened as if of its own accord and stayed wide ajar as he whooshed out of it and disappeared from Yadwiga's view. Having let Koshchei out, the door shut with a loud bang – and silence set in.

"Where are we?" Sergei asked his wife. He felt as if he had just woken up from a long sleep.

"I have no idea," said Irina.

Then they saw Granny Yadwiga discussing something in English with a police officer across the room. She finished talking and approached the Sablins.

"Well, I've sorted it all out," she announced. "A small misunderstanding about your Underground fare. I have explained to the officer here that it was your ever first Tube journey, paid off the difference – and the matter is now closed. We should hurry back home, for Olga and Danya must be very worried!"

"How are we going to get back?" asked Irina. "I am not going back on the Tube, not for a million pounds!"

"It is too late for the Tube anyway," said Yadwiga. "Besides, London has taxis. And I've already called one. So let's come out of the building and wait for it. It must be on its way."

They went out of the station. It was pitch dark and very cold outside.

"The taxi's number plate will be AER 8," said Yadwiga. "So make sure we don't miss it."

It was a funny thing to say: there were neither people nor cars anywhere in sight.

Sergei, who was feeling nippy and was bouncing on the spot to warm up, suddenly heard a whining mechanical noise from above and looked up. An old jalopy of a car – so ancient it must have been made well before World War II – was descending upon them from the dark sky, its headlights aglow. Dazed as Sergei was by the sight, he couldn't help noticing that the jalopy's driving seat was empty.

He looked at Irina, who was so startled that she was unable to utter a word.

"Haven't you heard of the famous London flying cabs?" asked Yadwiga as the car landed next to them and all its four doors opened invitingly. "Here's one. Don't be shy, get inside!"

It was of course a bit of an indulgence on Yadwiga's part. But after all the troubles of the day and after her surprise victory over Koshchei, she couldn't deny herself and the Sablins a little treat. There was of course a risk of them guessing who she really was. But – like in numerous other instances – she had an easy remedy for it: to make them forget. Her own flying kit was missing, and flying back astride Snake Horinich was not an option for all three of them: cold, not very comfortable and too scary for the Sablins. So before entering the police station, she had managed to commandeer AER 8 from 127, Woodville Avenue. AER stood for "Astral Energy Receiver" – a sort of a charger for witches' flying utensils, be they brooms or vacuum cleaners. But during the night, when the demand for astral energy was not too high, it could double as a car and a taxi.

"What are you waiting for? Get in!" repeated Yadwiga. Sergei and Irina obeyed – and seconds later they were all hovering in the black starless sky above North London. The giant city was asleep, yet myriads of street lights were still blinking below like little stars. With no proper stars in the sky, it suddenly started looking to Sergei and Irina as if their whole world had turned upside down and they were no longer able to tell where reality ended and a fairy tale began.

Looking at them, Yadwiga could not help smiling.

"What a curious thing – human nature," she was thinking. "They will forget all about it later, but for now – I will let them enjoy the flight!"

Chapter Eleven

In which the Sablins learn English by the "immersion method", Koshchei poses as a female student and Humphrey Smith gets a surprise delivery

"WHAT are we doing here? I am freezing!" moaned Olga. "Indeed, why was it so urgent to come to this forest so early in the morning?" echoed Irina.

"Stop questioning me this very moment!" roared Yadwiga. "You will find it all out very soon!"

"Girls, please be quiet, will you? Granny Yadwiga wouldn't have brought us here, had it not been important!" It was Sergei trying to pacify his wife and daughter, not an easy task having in mind the time of this conversation – seven o'clock in the morning – and the place – Highgate Ponds in the middle of Hampstead Heath, a vast park and forest in North London.

The Sablins – both senior and junior – had hardly had time to recover after yesterday's ordeal, with Danya and Olga waking up late at night, hungry and confused, to the sight of Granny Yadwiga and their parents returning home after a long absence and unable to provide a coherent account of where they had been and of how they had got back.

And yet, hardly had they gone to sleep when Granny woke them all up again saying they had to do something very important and a taxi was waiting outside. She then brought them to this deserted forest at the break of dawn. But the most worrisome part of this unlikely morning adventure – from the Sablins' point of view – was Yadwiga insisted on all of them wearing swim suits underneath their winter coats. In January! Even Danya was somewhat puzzled by this demand of his beloved Granny and was hoping against hope that it was a warm indoor swimming pool they were heading for.

All the way to the Heath – in the car and, later, when they were trudging through the dark forest – neither Yadwiga nor the Sablins uttered a single word. It was only when they stopped on the bank of the Men's Pond – one of the three swimming ponds on Hampstead Heath – that first Olga and then Irina broke the silence.

The water in the pond was uninviting, to say the least: black, rippled and covered by a thin icy crust here and there. The sky above them was also hostile and resembled a thick tarpaulin hood: impenetrably black, with just a few timid touches of grey in one corner. And the bare, leafless trees were rustling above their heads threateningly…

"Now, listen to me," Yadwiga said finally. "I am sorry for bringing you here at this early hour and even more sorry for what I am going to ask you to do now. You may have guessed what it is…"

"I am not going for a swim! Not for a million dollars!" shouted Olga.

"Not for a swim, but for a quick dive – that's all I want!" Yadwiga retorted and carried on: "You have probably never heard of the world's best and quickest way of learning a foreign language – the 'immersion method'. They say it was invented in Canada and further developed in Bulgaria by Lozanov, a local teacher – but that is not the whole story. I found out about this method long before Lozanov, and took it one step further: from immersion to submersion. 'Submersion' is about throwing the student into the foreign-speaking environment – head first, rather than immersing him into it gradually – and leaving him there, not dissimilar to when a person who cannot swim is thrown into a pond or a river. In this situation, he or she will have little choice but to learn how to swim – and fast. It can work the same way with language, as I myself found out many years ago – just here, on Hampstead Heath – with the help of a friend of mine, who was a famous English writer. It is important to know where to be immersed. Try and plunge into any pond in Slavonia or even into the River Thames here in Britain – and nothing will happen. Apart from you getting soaked, that is, and probably catching a cold too.

"But these ponds here have some amazing qualities, being all fed by the headwater springs of the Fleet – an underground London river. On the surface, the river simply does not exist any longer. But it is here, on Hampstead Heath, that this non-existent river comes up for air and forms these ponds – the only place where one can actually get immersed it its miraculous underground waters flowing from the past, as if coming from an imaginary country called Yesterdayland, the country where everything is possible… I had the chance to feel their magic, if somewhat icy, touch on my skin years ago – and since then my English has been as good as if I were born and bred here. Now think how much time, money and effort you are going to save by a quick dive into this pond!"

The Sablins stayed silent.

"You may have noticed my dislike of questions, no matter how timely and logical they may sound," continued Yadwiga. "But at this point I would expect you to ask why foreigners aren't queuing up to have a dip in these miraculous ponds? And I will answer: because simply diving is not enough. While underwater, we have to awaken our magical ear – we all have one, only most people never come to discover it. It is this very ear that makes us sensitive, at times super-sensitive, to music, to the sounds of nature and to languages too. There is a very powerful mantra to help you awaken the magical ear by activating your larynx chakra, and it keeps changing every day depending on the position of the stars. Today it is: '*AUM CHIVATUN Eeeee!*' You have to pronounce it silently but clearly in your head while staying completely submerged. '*AUM CHIVATUN Eeeee!*' Please repeat it after me."

"*AUM CHIVATUN Eeeee!*" the Sablins chanted reluctantly.

Sergei began unbuttoning his coat.

"I look forward to this swim!" he announced. "The water must not be half as cold as in Slavonia, where as a student I belonged to a

'Walrus' society. We used to plunge into ice-holes in winter – and I never caught a cold! Doctors say that icy water is good for blood circulation!"

"It well may be, but I'd still rather do it in summer and during the day, not first thing in the morning," muttered Irina.

"There are reasons for doing it here and now," said Yadwiga. "Firstly, you cannot live, let alone work, in this country with no English, as you probably realise after yesterday's adventures. Secondly, even in the dark, you must have noticed the ropes that enclose the pond's swimming area. They only remove them in mid-April when the water temperature reaches twelve degrees, until then swimming in the ponds is not allowed for anyone who is not a member of the local swimmers' club. But you simply cannot wait that long, and, to avoid possible confrontation with the rangers, or, Gardner forbid, with police – you don't need another one after yesterday's! – I decided that the best time to do it would be early morning when bumping into anyone else in this forest, even the ubiquitous dog walkers, is fairly unlikely. That is why, although it is normally the Men's Pond, it should be OK for the ladies to dip in too… But enough talking. Let's get it over and done with, as they say in England. In and out within a second! You won't have time to feel the cold. But make sure you get submerged completely for as long as it takes you to say '*AUM CHIVATUN Eeeee!*' Otherwise, the method won't work!"

All the Sablins, including Danya, were already shivering on the water edge in their swimming costumes.

"When I say '*trea*,' move back the ropes and jump in head-first!" commanded Yadwiga. "*Odin… dva… tree-ea!!!*"

Four splashes – three very loud and one less so from Danya – were followed by four ear-piercing screams, and within a second or two all four of them were back on the ground rubbing themselves frantically with large fluffy towels, miraculously produced by Yadwiga from thin wintry air.

"That was so cool!" shouted Danya in English.

"It was super!" agreed Olga and added hastily: "I nearly forgot the mantra, but remembered it at the very last moment, and now – yippee! – I am speaking English too!"

"I feel fit as a fiddle!" Sergei laughed out loud.

"Lo and behold, what a great fleeting moment in the Fleet – forgive my pun!" commented Irina with a slight North London accent.

Standing aside and holding a spare towel, Yadwiga could feel tears of joy filling up her eyes.

"From now on – no more Slavonian!" she announced. "And let's get moving: it's going to be light soon!"

* * *

Yadwiga could be forgiven for thinking that not a single human being had been able to spot the Sablins' "immersion" (or was it "submersion"?) in the pond. And she was right in a way, for he who did see them was certainly not human – in more than one sense. It was Koshchei the Deathless who had the powers of both night and distant vision. On this occasion, however, the distance was actually not that huge, for he was watching the Sablins from the top of the central turret of Athlone House – a detached Victorian pile in the shape of a medieval castle on the hill overlooking the Heath. Built in 1871, the eclectic red brick house with imitation Gothic turrets and spires, also known as Caen Wood Towers, had a number of owners and at different times functioned as a military hospital and a nurses' training school until it fell into disrepair and now stood abandoned and awaiting restoration. It was ideal for Koshchei as a temporary London abode, and he was unable to contain a nasty chuckle while watching the Sablins' initiation into English. With his radar-like hearing, he could catch every word they were saying. "That despicable Baron Lytton," he thought when he heard Yadwiga mention "her English writer friend." "It was not enough for him to take Yadwiga away from me, now he is threatening my immortality from the grave!"

Koshchei had already had his revenge on Bulwer-Lytton by using his spells to make nearly everyone forget about him. As a result, Britain's most famous and prolific author of the second half of the nineteenth century, whose books regularly outsold Dickens', fell into nearly total obscurity after 1914 – to the extent that he hadn't even been included in a single Penguin anthology of English classics! But Koshchei did not stop there. He knew that the only thing worse than oblivion was ridicule, and, in 1982, he managed to persuade a native American shaman from San Jose, who owed him a small favour and a crate of whisky from the times of Prohibition, to launch the Bulwer-Lytton Fiction Contest for the worst opening sentence of a novel, using the writer's proverbial "It was a dark and stormy night…" from *Paul Clifford* as a sample. In reality, there was nothing particularly awful about that opening sentence, it was actually rather colourful and descriptive, but the shaman did a good job, and the contest quickly grew popular in America and then internationally, despite the fact that the prize for winning it was pitiful – $250! All over the world people were now laughing at Bulwer-Lytton, and Koshchei himself, who normally detested poetry, came up with the following doggerel:

Oblivion is every writer's curse,

But mockery, my friends, is even worse!

"My friends" was of course poetic licence, because Koshchei didn't have any.

Friends or no friends, Bulwer-Lytton's name and reputation had been effectively destroyed. Koshchei would have been even happier to erase from humankind's memory all Bulwer-Lytton's books, particularly *Zanoni*, but that was beyond his powers: all the black magic in the world is helpless against a true work of literature.

On reflection, Koshchei decided to forget about Yadwiga and the Sablins for the moment and to deal with them later. The priority now was to explore that "old bookshop in Covent Garden" once again. Koshchei knew exactly what Bulwer-Lytton meant – Melissa's Runes bookshop in Bloomsbury, the area which in the mid-nineteenth century was still too unfashionable and too insignificant to feature in a book as a separate location and was therefore referred to as Covent Garden, of which it had always been a part. Having heard the rumours of a corridor that could lead to the hiding place of the egg with his death inside it a long time ago, he had made several attempts to find it by entering the shop first as himself and then under different guises, but Melissa, who hated him more than Yadwiga and Lucinda combined, had always been able to unmask his true self and throw him out. Yesterday's confrontation with Yadwiga at Totteridge Police Station made it absolutely clear to Koshchei that it was time to give it another try: the knowledge of the magic corridor was spreading fast – and that yet unwritten *Granny Yaga* book was a real worry – so he simply had no choice but to get there first and defuse the situation by taking the egg and re-hiding it properly before anyone else could reach it.

Usually Koshchei had little problem getting inside any house or any premises, no matter how well they were guarded and how thoroughly locked, yet the Runes bookshop was protected by Melissa's own strong spells. Koshchei knew that Yadwiga's *yagishna sister was a powerful ved'ma*, and it was impossible to simply sneak past her into the shop. He had to be inventive, and now he was conjuring up a different plan, both daring and simple. On numerous occasions, Koshchei had tried to get into the shop's basement, where the magic doorway was allegedly located, disguised as a gas meter reader, a burglar, a postman or a much-dreaded Camden Council Hygiene and Standards inspector, but all in vain. Could it be simply because all the above characters were male, he was wondering?

As the world's greatest magician, Koshchei could turn into anything or anyone, and this time he decided to change tactics and to pose as a young woman in the hope that Melissa wouldn't make the connection between his old male self and a young female customer!

To succeed, Koshchei had to act differently from the start, so that morning, instead of flying, he took the Tube to Holborn. Having emerged from the Underground, he crossed the road and walked towards Bloomsbury Square with a crowd of Le Cordon Bleu Culinary Academy students anxious to be in time for a demonstration class. They were in a hurry, for if you were a little late for this class, the teaching chef could mark you as absent – and several absences could mean failing the whole course. In his star-spangled cloak and cone-shaped wizard's hat, Koshchei himself could pass for a slightly eccentric elderly chef who taught at the school.

In Southampton Row, his tall hat got blown off and carried away by the wind. Koshchei caught up with it and was about to pick it up when Hooey Wong, bespectacled student from China, who was the first to spot Baba Yaga in the sky above Bloomsbury two days earlier, bumped into him, dropped her glasses and muttered: "I am sorry!" It was at that very moment that the chef-like old man in a funny tunic suddenly disappeared, as if he fell through the ground, and Hooey Wong, having picked up her glasses, straightened her dress and continued her progress towards Bloomsbury. Only instead of the new school building in Bloomsbury Square, she headed for a side lane off Museum Street where the Runes bookshop was located.

The moment she moved away from the collision spot, another Hooey Wong – an exact copy of the first one, stood up from the ground, picked up her glasses and, having straightened her dress, ran towards Bloomsbury Square to be in time for the demonstration class.

Melissa was about to open up the shop and was lifting a heavy iron shutter from the front window when she saw in it a reflection of a young Asian girl, most likely a student. The girl looked shy and slightly baffled.

Melissa turned towards her: "Can I help you?"

"Is this the famous Runes bookshop?" asked the girl and added: "I am sorry, my eyesight is not brilliant and I cannot read the sign." She spoke with a strong foreign accent and appeared genuine.

"Well, I am not sure about the famous bit, but it is definitely the shop you are after," said Melissa. "Come on in. You are my first customer today."

The girl entered the shop and for a minute or so studied the wall poster advertising a forthcoming talk by "Juanita Puddifoot, founder and creator of 'Energy Gateways' – a way of working that focuses on the Subtle Energy Fields of Life." She then walked up to the counter nearest to the entrance and, ignoring several back issues of "Pagan Dawn" magazine displayed on it, picked up a copy of the "Handbook of Practical Magic" by Samael Aun Weor and started reading.

"How strange: she was complaining of bad eyesight but is not even using reading glasses," thought Melissa before attributing the girl's unusual behaviour to her innate oriental shyness.

"Is there anything in particular you are after?" she asked.

The girl looked up from the book.

"I come from Communist China, the country where witches are persecuted and anything connected with magic or religion is either banned or frowned upon," she blurted out. "But I have always taken interest in the occult, particularly in the *wu* tradition and its connection with *fangshi* as well as in Taoism and Confucianism. I wonder if you have anything on the *I Ching* system of divination and the *Pa Kua?*"

"I am sorry, but we do not really specialise in oriental philosophies," said Melissa. "The only thing I can offer you is an old book of hexagram combinations illustrating the balance of *yin* and *yang*. But it will take some time to find it in the storage room. Also, this old volume is rare and therefore expensive – it will set you back eighty-five pounds…"

"This is excellent!" the girl clapped her hands. "I think I can afford it. My father is Chief Engineer of a large car factory in Nanking!"

"Very well, then. You can wait here. Would you like a soft drink or a coffee while you are waiting?"

"No, thank you very much, I am fine!"

The storage room door was behind the till in the far corner of the shop.

"Can you please ring this bell on my desk if another customer comes in?" said Melissa.

"No problem, ma'am!" replied the girl, alias Koshchei, who had already spotted a narrow staircase leading to the basement. The moment Melissa disappeared inside the storage room, he ran towards it. He was expecting to find a curtained door or at least a dark cave-like recess leading to the tunnel at the bottom of the stairs, but there was nothing. The only thing he could see in the murky light of a solitary light bulb was a solid concrete wall with no doors or curtains.

"Disappointed, Koshchei?" Melissa's angry voice roared behind his back. A technologically savvy *ved'ma*, she had CCTV cameras all over the shop and could see "the girl" dash down the stairs the moment she closed the storage room door behind her.

He was exposed and it was no longer necessary to carry on with the camouflage. The girl's oriental face and her short figure got blurred and curiously elongated before melting away in the stale air of the basement – and Koshchei was back to his normal looks: thin, stooping and with a silly pointed hat on his head.

"I know what you were looking for," continued Melissa. "And you are right: there is a doorway somewhere. But opening it requires a magic password, known to just one person – Lord Bulwer-Lytton himself who, as we all know, died in January 1873. So you'd better get out of here as fast as your long old legs can carry you and never come back!"

For the second time in less than a day Koshchei was defeated. Only on this occasion he didn't feel like arguing with Melissa or even like talking back. With his head lowered almost to the level of the sharp upturned tips of his fancy morocco shoes, he limped up the stairs.

"Next time, I will try to get in here as a cat. Or as rat," he was thinking on his way out of the shop and back into the street.

* * *

"Who is that again?" Humphrey Smith, deputy head of the British Museum's Pre-History Department, looked with disgust at the telephone ringing on his desk, which he had just finished tidying up. It was the end of his last day at the office before a short, yet long-awaited and much-needed, holiday in Majorca, where he and his wife Sarah were flying the following morning. It was only a five-day break, for he had to be back at work for the opening of the exhibition "East European Folklore: Images and Symbols," of which he was a curator. He was about to leave when the phone rang.

It was a security guard from the downstairs lobby saying that a woman who refused to introduce herself or leave any contact details had just delivered a set of curious objects to the main reception which might interest him.

"We have checked them for explosives and other booby traps, and they are clean," the guard assured him and added: "But they... they... behave in a strange manner..."

"Who? The objects behave strangely? You cannot be serious! OK, I'll be down shortly," said Humphrey Smith angrily. He decided he'd have a look at those misbehaving objects on his way out of the building.

Yet when he made his way through a thick crowd of late visitors flocking around the reception desk, he realised he was not going to leave the office any time soon. A large elongated mortar was hanging in the air half a metre above the reception desk, as if suspended from the ceiling. Only it had no strings attached to it. And next to the mortar, an old dishevelled broom and a worn out pestle were hovering peacefully. It didn't take him long to authenticate the objects as a typical Baba Yaga's flying kit. He also thought he could recognise it from the vision of the flying old woman he was exposed to the other evening – the sight that both he and Sarah hurried to dismiss as a hallucination caused by over-exhaustion.

The three objects were dancing in the air playfully, as if inviting him to pick them up. Or maybe even offering a ride?

"Please go home, the museum is closed!" he announced to the crowd of onlookers. "These are just some new animatronic exhibits for our forthcoming folklore exhibition, so you can all come back in a week and have a proper look at them!"

And to himself he thought: "Why not? Whatever they are and whoever delivered them – they will cause a sensation. Majorca will have to wait!"

He could almost see a PhD thesis with his name on the front page, levitating above the reception desk, next to the Baba Yaga's tools.

Chapter Twelve

In which Danya visits the British Museum and Koshchei comes up with a devious plan

FOUR and a half months after the Hampstead Heath "immersion", the lives of all five members of the Sablin family – including Yadwiga, of course – had changed beyond recognition.

The children were going to school: Danya to Fordington Primary down the road; Olga to Pages Lane Secondary in Muswell Hill. They were both doing well and were enjoying their studies, although, in Danya's opinion, there was too much play and not enough learning, and the discipline was more relaxed compared to his last school in Slavonia. He also discovered that he was much more advanced in some subjects, particularly in maths, than his classmates, which showed that a strictly disciplinarian approach had its positive sides too. To keep himself challenged, he joined an afternoon taekwondo class held in the school's gym twice a week, and very quickly earned himself the first belt, the yellow one.

Olga was excelling at her school, too, and was a popular girl, despite being occasionally teased for her posh accent. She particularly liked music lessons, was very good at playing guitar and was invited to join the all-girl rock band, for which she also invented (with a bit of help from Granny Yadwiga) a name – "Lady Yaga" – to echo the famous pop star Lady Gaga, although none of the other girls in the band knew what "Yaga" stood for.

Irina found a part-time job at "Kashtan", a small and cosy East European delicatessen on Talbot Parade one Tube stop away from Woodville Avenue. Apart from starchy East European food and strong drinks, the deli had a tiny books section, which – helped by Irina's love and knowledge of literature – saw a massive increase in sales to the sheer delight of the shop's Indian owner.

Sergei – on Yadwiga's advice – placed a short "Home Repairs" ad, which he had put together himself, in a local weekly newsletter:

Reliable handyman. Total renovations. Kitchens, bathrooms, tiling, plumbing.

The response exceeded his expectations: he had lots of customers, particularly after he acquainted himself with the intricacies of the British plumbing system which, as he quickly discovered, was almost as outdated and ineffective as Slavonia's. On top of this, he managed to fix Pani Czerniowiecka's old boiler, which was deranged and chronically malfunctioning, so she would be in for a pleasant surprise on her next return from the grave, which was due soon. Rumours of Sergei's skills quickly spread all over the area and he was often hired by residents of the neighbouring Woodville Avenue houses, with the exception of number 127, from which strange noises could sometimes be heard.

As for Yadwiga, she had two major breakthroughs. Firstly, she opened a Yesterdayland portal in the crypts of St Etheldreda's Chapel in Ely Place, and that allowed her to reinstall the time firewall between Yesterday and Today. She then safely moved her old Hut to the Elm Tree Wood Cottage, so that its new owners would never be able to notice that they were sharing their house with an old lady and her cat, for they lived in Today, not in Yesterdayland, and those two were now completely separate! Bulgakov was finally able to return to his favourite pastime: lying on the stove and reading books – both published ones and those that hadn't been written yet.

Snake Horinich felt at home in his spacious Yesterdayland garage inside the abandoned Victorian pile next to the playground in Elm Tree Wood. Local kids, supervised by their mummies and nannies, would have been very surprised, perhaps even frightened, to find out what sort of creature was hiding in the house next to the place where they played. But there was no chance of that whatsoever, with the time firewall firmly in place.

When not inside his garage, Snake Horinich would spend more and more time on the roof of house number 125 sitting in for its resident little dragon, whose absences to "stretch his wings" were getting longer and more frequent since he met a pretty she-dragon in the murky skies above Dollis Hill. He soon set up a new home with his seemingly loveable dragoness, who had two beautiful fiery heads and three green, scaled torsos (her third head was bitten off in a fight with another North West London she-dragon and hadn't grown back yet). This flying love story quickly came to a tragic finale when the mutilated body of the little red dragon, with both wings torn off, was found in Dollis Creek and mistaken for that of an alligator – all the local residents can verify it! So Snake Horinich had to replace his one-headed friend on the roof on a semi-permanent basis, commuting between his garage and house number 125 – and therefore between Yesterdayland and Today.

As well as Snake Horinich, the three Horsemen were also occasionally allowed to leave Yesterdayland, mostly at dusk or at dawn, so that their horses could graze on the juicy Elm Tree Wood meadows of Today that stayed emerald green even in winter but would naturally lose some of their freshness and colour in Yesterdayland.

Yadwiga celebrated the opening of the Ely Place portal in the nearby Devil's Tavern at 2, Fleet Street in the company of Melissa and Pani Czerniowiecka, who managed to leave her Highgate Cemetery sarcophagus for an evening on that occasion. The Devil's Tavern was officially demolished in 1787, but – unbeknown to the City of Westminster licensing authorities – it continued to exist and to thrive in Yesterdayland.

After that celebration, on Melissa's advice and with some help from "Witch Flier" magazine, Yadwiga acquired a Dyson to replace her lost mortar and pestle. To her own surprise, she was enjoying her new "smart" flying vehicle, with its GPS, liquid crystal monitors and an embedded custom-made Koshchei sensor.

Yadwiga did need a vehicle – old or new – to take her around as she had a couple of rather pressing matters to attend to: to find Lucinda and to establish whether her old friend Baron Lytton was indeed dead, or not quite so and hence able to reveal the magic password for the invisible doorway inside Melissa's shop.

* * *

Danya did not want to go on this school trip from the start, as if he knew it would end badly. But there was little he could do to avoid this visit to the British Museum's new exhibition on East European folklore. His whole class was going, and, as Miss Sharpe, the deputy headmistress and their history teacher, herself said on the eve of the visit, Sablin (that was Danya) should be able to guide them through the exhibits, for it was, as she put it, "his own heritage and part of the world he himself had come from." How could he opt out of it after such a statement?

On the morning of the visit, a specially booked coach was waiting in the street outside the school – and soon they were on the way to Bloomsbury.

A long queue was snaking out of the museum gate, but as a school group on a pre-booked organised tour, they were able to jump it.

"Children, we are honoured to have Mr Humphrey Smith, the exhibition's curator, as our guide," Miss Sharpe announced and added somewhat mischievously: "I have personally asked him to take us around and he was unable to deny this little favour to his old university friend!"

Inside a vast semi-dark exhibition hall, they were greeted by Humphrey Smith himself: "Helen, it is my pleasure to welcome you and your students!" he said with a broad smile.

To Danya, he looked very scholarly, even academic – with a bow tie underneath a tweed jacket and grey designer stubble on his cheeks.

And the tour began.

"This is the biggest and the most comprehensive exhibition on East European folklore ever held on British soil, numbering hundreds of objects, some of which are truly unique…"

Humphrey Smith led the children to the first set of exhibits: a row of glass cases with an array of brightly lit maps and paintings above them.

"This part of the exhibition is reserved for supernatural beings, with which East European folklore is resplendent. Some of them might sound familiar to you, like, for example, *rusalki* – mermaid-like female creatures, only, unlike our mermaids who dwell in seas, they mostly inhabit lakes and rivers. Many of the *rusalki* represent women murdered by their lovers, and, although dead, they are not always scary and vicious. Unlike mermaids, they do not have fish tails and are often rather beautiful, even if sad, as you can see in this painting by Polish artist Witold Pruszkowski.

The painting on the wall showed two ghostly pale-faced young women with wreaths made of flowers on their heads.

"It is interesting that many East European folklore characters are associated with water," Humphrey Smith continued. "Among them is a male equivalent of the *rusalka* called *vodianoi* or *wodnik* in Polish. Unlike the *rusalka*, he is invariably vicious and is notorious for drowning swimmers who have angered him with their loud splashes or by venturing too far into his domain . Some folklore tales define him as a green naked old man, bloated and hairy, covered in slime or in scales, and capable of transforming into a fish. In short, not an attractive creature…"

"I disagree!" shouted Sean Shadrake, Danya's ebullient classmate. "This Botnik, or whatever you call him, sounds cool and wicked to me!"

"Not if you bump into him in a swimming pool during a PE lesson, although he might indeed feel cold to the touch," Miss Sharpe commented wryly. She was popular among Fordington Primary pupils for her dry, if somewhat cruel, sense of humour.

They came up to an old engraving featuring a young woman – either in a shroud or in a very loose nightgown – whose torso was above the ground, whereas the lower parts of her body were firmly inside a grave.

"This nineteenth-century engraving by Polish artist Jan Styfi shows a very peculiar folklore character that has no analogues in Western mythology," Humphrey Smith announced solemnly. "Called *dziwozona*, or *mamuna*, she is a female demon who is neither alive nor dead but something in between. That is why she is portrayed in her habitual half-buried state here."

Danya thought the semi-dead woman looked spooky and turned away from the "engraving," a word that had suddenly acquired a sinister – grave-related – connection.

Humphrey Smith noticed Danya's reaction.

"Not all East European folklore characters are so gruesome," he said with a smile. "Many are much more cheerful and life-enhancing, like, for example, a woodland spirit called *leshiy* or *lesovyk*; *perelesnyk* – a spirit of seduction; *volkodlak* – a Magi sorcerer who can cause sun eclipses; *chugaister* – a forest giant; *niavka* – a woodland nymph; or *mara* – a rather facetious spirit of confusion who deprives wanderers of their sense of direction and makes them lost in a forest – just for fun... Ahem... Getting lost in an East European forest can be funny indeed, unless you come across the most colourful fairy-tale personage: Baba Yaga Bony Legs. Why Bony Legs, you may ask? Because, in spite of her ferocious appetite, particularly for children, that old hag is as thin as a rake. She lives in a hut on extra-large chicken legs which seems to have a personality of their own In some stories she has two sisters, who are sometimes called Baba Yaga as well, just to confuse you, and sometimes called *yagishnas*. Baba Yaga's nose is so long that it rattles against the ceiling of her hut when she snores..."

"These are all lies!" Danya shouted all of a sudden. "Baba Yaga is not ugly, her nose is not that long and she doesn't eat children!"

He immediately regretted his outburst, but it was too late.

Humphrey Smith was staring at him in amazement, his mouth agape, while his classmates burst out laughing.

"Children, please behave yourselves!" intervened Miss Sharpe. "Danny Sablin comes from Eastern Europe, so he knows these fairy tales better than you do, and his perception of some of the characters can be different from ours!"

"Helen is right," said Humphrey Smith. "The interesting thing about Baba Yaga is that she is probably the most ambiguous, meaning controversial, folklore character ever. She is not entirely bad, not at all, and in some fairy tales she can actually be a positive force too – not just a creature of darkness. She is also in charge of the three Horsemen symbolising night, day and sun. She also sticks to her word and if a visiting maiden does everything as she says, she never eats her up! This double nature is very well portrayed in the famous drawing by the brilliant artist Ivan Bilibin, of which we have the original here."

He led the pupils to a vignette-style painting featuring Baba Yaga – sullen and dishevelled – sitting inside a mortar.

"Indeed, Baba Yaga is unusual." The curator carried on pointing at the painting. "Unlike your average Western witch, she doesn't wear a silly pointed hat, nor does she ever travel astride a broomstick. Instead, she moves around the forest and flies above it perched in a large mortar, like this one in the painting, and pushes herself ahead with the pestle!"

Mesmerised by the expressive and colourful drawing and by the very idea of a flying mortar, the children went quiet.

"In fact, we have a very special treat for you here today," Humphrey Smith said mysteriously. "I am now going to ask our new security guard, Mr Atlas Halliday from America, to unlock for us a case with a very special exhibit, which is still being investigated by our researchers and therefore only shown to our most distinguished visitors. Your teacher, Miss Sharpe, or simply Helen to me, is certainly one of such distinguished people, and so are you all!"

Humphrey Smith pressed a button on the pager stuck to his belt – and in came Atlas Ex-Map Halliday in the black uniform of a security guard. He applied for the job shortly after the events described in Chapter One and was enjoying it immensely.

"Atlas, dear, could you kindly take us to room twenty-four and unlock the case in it?" Humphrey Smith asked him.

"Yes, sir!" replied Ex-Map Halliday, military-style. "Follow me, please!"

Having taken a large bunch of dangling keys out of his pocket, he led the group to a small door in the corner of the exhibition hall, unlocked it and invited everyone inside. In the centre of the room stood a large cube-shaped glass case, covered with black tarpaulin.

Atlas removed the tarpaulin, and everybody in the room gasped: inside the case, Yadwiga's old mortar and pestle were hovering – floating in the air half a metre above the floor, as if warming up (which they were, for they needed exercise!) and inviting everyone for a ride (which they weren't).

"These are my Granny's!" That was Danya again, unable to control his emotions.

His outcry triggered another bout of loud laughter from his classmates, with Sean Shadrake laughing the loudest.

"What are you talking about?" Humphrey Smith and Miss Sharpe cried out in astonishment.

"It is my Granny Yadwiga's flying kit! I know because I've had a ride in it!" Danya's joy at having found the mortar and the pestle which, as Granny herself had confided in him, had been stolen from her, was too huge for him to control.

"Listen to him!" shouted Sean Shadrake. "He must have lost his marbles! I suggest we start calling him Dan the Loony from now on!"

"Stop the bullying!" commanded Miss Sharpe while realising very clearly that from now on Danya's bullying would be increasingly hard to contain. "Danny was just trying to be funny, weren't you Danny? I thought it was a hilarious comment. But now it's time to go back. The bus is waiting outside!"

Still giggling, the children trailed towards the exit.

"Can I have a quick word?" Humphrey Smith pulled Danya by the sleeve and took him aside.

"That Granny of yours…" he whispered. "Could you please tell her to get in touch with me ASAP? I may have a very nice surprise waiting for her!"

Humphrey did it on the spur of the moment, for the boy did not appear insane to him. At least, no more insane than he himself felt when he saw the flying Baba Yaga in the sky above the British Museum several months earlier.

* * *

Koshchei was triumphant.

The solution came to him the previous night when he was watching the ten o'clock BBC TV news inside his temporary London abode – the top of the central turret of Athlone House in Hampstead Heath. A bright log fire was burning inside an enormous fireplace in front of the vast Biedermeier couch on which he was reclining. Log fires were strictly banned anywhere in Greater London, but Koshchei's antique fireplace – old just like this whole London shelter of his – remained invisible to ordinary humans and therefore outside the scope of the London authorities' regulations.

At the end of the news bulletin, there came a short sports roundup. The news was to be followed by Match of the Day, a football programme which would normally contain reports of the most important Premier League games. That was why the news presenter suggested matter-of-factly that those viewers who didn't want to know the results should look away from the screen and cover up their ears.

On hearing the announcement, Koshchei jumped up from the armchair screaming: "Eureka!"

For days in a row he had been thinking about how to outwit Yadwiga and Melissa and be the first to get hold of the egg with his life (and death) inside it, of which he had lost track several hundred years before, so that he could re-hide it in a safe place known to him – and to him, alone! His deathlessness would then be guaranteed for ever and ever. Until the previous night, he could see only two ways of beating Yadwiga to the secret underground passageway, where – as he had reason to believe – the egg was hidden: to find out Bulwer-Lytton's password himself or to get it out of Lucinda, one of the three *yagishna* sisters who possessed the amazing gift of clairvoyance. Neither of these seemed realistic: Koshchei himself had very little chance of cracking the old Baron's code – how could he, when he had never had anything in common with the man, apart for their shared passion for young Yadwiga? As for getting the clue from Lucinda, well, he had to track her down first which could prove difficult and time-consuming, whereas Yadwiga, whom he had made to age considerably but who still retained her natural intelligence and quick wit, would probably guess it much, much faster. He could of course wait for Yadwiga to find the clue and then try to force it out of her, but realised that she would rather die there and then than spill it out.

Yet the moment he heard the TV presenter's call on those who did not want to know the results of the games, which HAD ALREADY happened, to cover their ears, he could clearly see a third way.

If that book, *Granny Yaga*, indeed existed, as Yadwiga had assured him, the author should know the clue and should put it on paper before anyone else uncovers it! To wait for Yadwiga – or any other character from this book, including Koshchei himself – to be told the password by the writer was like covering one's ears and turning away from the TV screen to shield yourself from something that was already a *fait accompli* – an accomplished fact! It was like burying your head in the sand, ostrich-like, and choosing ignorance over a reality which could prove unpleasant, yes, but is destined to catch up with you anyway, sooner or later.

Perhaps, for humans, with their short life span, this sort of logic sounded reasonable: it may be better NOT to know that your favourite team has lost the game for another hour or so and in the meantime to remain blissfully deluded that it might have won. You could also experience *belated* excitement while watching the recorded broadcast of your team losing nil to eight, or winning eight to nil. But the one thing you couldn't do is change the result, which was set in stone the moment the referee blew the final whistle. No recordings could alter it, so your excitement over something that had been over a long time ago was bound to be all but futile!

On the other hand, for an immortal creature, like Koshchei, with all the time in the world on his hands, temporary delusions – no matter how satisfying – did not make a lot of sense. So, if he could somehow get a sneak preview of the chapter in the book in which Yadwiga cracks Bulwer-Lytton's coded password (and knowing Yadwiga, Koshchei had little doubt that she would – and soon) and then distract her from acting it out immediately, he had a real chance of getting to the door – and to the egg – first!

Koshchei could hardly wait until the morning when he would be able to start translating his brilliant plan into reality. He had to wait until the Writer started a new chapter, number thirteen, of his *Granny Yaga* book. That could only happen the following morning, for to adjust the timing of the narrative to the book's characters, that very evening the Writer should still be busy describing Koshchei's own devious plan as it was unveiling in real time.

In short, Koshchei had to contain his ardour until the morning, but patience, the ability to wait, was among the main assets he had acquired during the many thousand years of his endless (or so he was inclined to think) life. Cackling happily and rubbing his long bony hands in glee, he sat in the armchair all through the night, staring at the TV screen and wishing that he possessed the ability to sleep, as some of the programmes were extremely tedious.

At about 4 a.m. when the first light of the early dawn glimmered above Hampstead Heath, Koshchei switched off his TV set – with considerable relief — climbed on top of the tower and took off towards a small town in Hertfordshire where the Writer lived.

He landed in a quiet leafy street a couple of hundred metres away from the Writer's house and promptly transformed himself into a squirrel — not a common grey squirrel, but a black one, endemic to that particular part of the UK. He waited behind a hedge for a couple of hours, then climbed up a tree and, jumping from one tree top to another, soon reached the Writer's spacious garden. He was in luck, for the Writer, with a pile of papers under his armpit, had just emerged from the back door of the house and, after stopping briefly at a wooden bird feeder to put some seeds in it, proceeded slowly towards Pegasus Cottage — his small and cosy garden office made of wood. Its name — Pegasus Cottage — was due to a rusty horseshoe the Writer once found on the roof of a garden shed that stood on the same spot, his rationale being that the only way a horseshoe could end up on the roof was if it had been dropped by the mythical flying horse, Pegasus. That was how Pegasus Cottage had come to replace the unremarkable garden shed.

The Writer's progress was deliberately unhurried, for he simultaneously cherished and loathed those moments of quiet before a day of hard work. "The most important thing for a writer is to learn not to recoil from a clean sheet of paper," was his favourite quote, which, in his opinion, neatly summed up all the controversies of the author's craft.

Having unlocked his writing shed, he lingered at its door for a moment or so — just enough for Koshchei, disguised as a black squirrel, to scurry inside and to hide behind a large tea kettle in the far corner of the vast Victorian desk.

From there he could see very clearly how the Writer, having reluctantly settled himself down in a tall office chair on wheels, switched on his laptop and entered a password so long and complicated that he only succeeded on the third go. With a jingle, the computer screen came to life, revealing neat rows of words and sentences of which Koshchei, who was now all eyes and ears, was able to discern every single letter. With a deep sigh, as if detesting profoundly the very process of writing, the Writer slowly typed in the first words of the day.

Chapter Thirteen

In which Yadwiga cracks Bulwer-Lytton's coded password and Pani Czerniowiecka returns from the grave

TO BE honest, Yadwiga was not seriously expecting to find Baron Lytton alive in any form. She knew that all his life he had been obsessed with immortality and at some point even delved into alchemy to find an elixir of eternal life, but – he while being a great writer – was not a strong enough magician to achieve it. Also, one had to be properly dead to be buried in Westminster Abbey, as Bulwer-Lytton was in 1873. At that world-famous pantheon, they must conduct numerous checks on the body to make sure that the demise is both serious and, well, truly terminal… Yet she did cherish some hope that before dying Bulwer-Lytton had left a clue as to how to access the magic passageway of which he gave more or less precise whereabouts in *Zanoni*.

The most obvious password would of course be *Vril* – the word invented by Bulwer-Lytton in his novel *The Coming Race* to denote the magic energy that fed the *Vril-ya*, the superior winged race populating an underground utopian land. Literary scholars have been wondering for years what could have prompted Bulwer-Lytton to come up with such an un-English-sounding, tongue-breaking word in the first place. It was only Yadwiga who knew the truth: the hard-to-pronounce *Vril-ya* was suggested to Edward by her as a rhyming analogue to the Slavonian word *kril'ya* – "wings". She did it in a letter in 1871, two years before Bulwer-Lytton's death, when their whirlwind romance had been over for many years, but they were still friends.

So popular was *The Coming Race* that the word *Vril* later evolved into a popular British trademark – Bovril – a beef extract used for food flavouring. Having it as a password would have been much too obvious for anyone familiar with Bulwer-Lytton's work. In vain did Yadwiga and Melissa take turns to utter: "*Vril!*" "*Vril!*" – both loudly and in a whisper – in front of the solid and seemingly impregnable concrete wall in the basement of the Runes bookshop. Unlike Yadwiga's own Hut on chicken feet, which would start turning on hearing the magic mantra ("Hut, Hut! Stand the way your mother placed you – with your back to the forest, your front to me"), the wall did not budge or move an inch.

Having thought it over, Yadwiga decided that if a clue indeed existed, she should be looking for it at Knebworth, Edward's Hertfordshire country house, where he had spent most of his life and which she herself had briefly visited in 1843, seven years after he divorced his wife, Rosina. She flew all the way from Slavonia (long before it became the USELES) to support Edward after the death of his beloved mother, Elizabeth, whom he had adored deeply and unconditionally – to the extent that, as he once admitted to Yadwiga, he felt at times as if he were his mum's favourite puppy (Elizabeth had always been surrounded by lapdogs for whom she had a long and enduring passion). Mrs Bulwer-Lytton was a formidable, if somewhat eccentric, lady. In her Regency-style bedroom, she had a false door to the right of her bed. That door led nowhere and was there for no reason other than symmetry. Yadwiga saw it with her own eyes when she entered the bedroom in which EBBL, as Edward's mum was commonly known (the initials of Elizabeth Barbara Bulwer-Lytton), was lying in state. Edward once confided in her that the false door in his mother's bedroom had given him the idea for the secret door inside the bookshop in his novel *Zanoni*.

In short, Yadwiga had reason to believe that she would be able to find some sort of a lead at Knebworth.

While still airborne, she couldn't help admiring the sheer size of Knebworth Park and estate: no wonder it was now one of Britain's largest public spaces, where open-air rock concerts were sometimes held for audiences of many thousands. She also noted how seemingly little the park and the house had changed in the nearly one hundred and seventy years since her last visit. She could even see the deer grazing on the lawn not far from the mansion – just like they did then. Of course the deer, as well as the present-day inhabitants of the house, were all different now, with a gap of many generations between them and those she saw during her previous stay. It was only the late Tudor building, with its quirky domes, turrets and towers, the pastoral landscape around it and Yadwiga herself that were still more or less the same, albeit – due to Koshchei's persisting curse – Yadwiga had aged considerably. Sitting astride her brand new, gleaming Dyson and clutching the hose, she suddenly felt tired and in need of rest.

There was little time for self-pity though. Yadwiga landed on a small lawn behind the car park and, having secured her Dyson with a padlock to a tree, lest it should be nicked like her previous flying kit (once bitten, twice shy), she mingled with the tourists that were making their way towards the house. She had to keep her eyes wide open for any sign left by Edward, and thought she saw one the moment she walked through a small wooden gate leading to the gardens. Opposite the gate stood a solitary and rather neglected sculpture of an angelic curly-haired young man, with a wreath on his head and a large bull-terrier-type dog at his feet. Despite the sculpture's peeling paint and its greyish time-beaten look, it was beautiful, and the dog – incongruous as it was – looked very much alive, as if ready to dash off and pounce at the passing tourists who didn't pay any attention to it. But remembering that Edward repeatedly referred to himself as his mum's puppy, Yadwiga did. "Maybe I should be looking for a dog or dogs," she was thinking as she read a strict and no doubt modern politically correct sign on the side of the manor house: "Dogs with the exception of guide dogs are not permitted." She looked up: countless scary-looking gargoyles (or were they chimeras?) were scowling at her from the roof. Some of them had distinctively dog-like snarls!

Yadwiga entered the house and, having shown her outrageously expensive £10.50 ticket to an elderly female attendant, found herself in a vast banqueting hall – less Gothic and less grand than she could recall, probably the result of the extensive early-twentieth-century renovations by famous British architect Sir Edwin Lutyens. Under the ceiling, along the perimeter of the hall, Edward's welcoming poem – a greeting to all visitors – was written, or rather painted, in large calligraphic letters. More dogs were in the family photos of the Cobbolds, the present-day owners of Knebworth, displayed on the table in one of the hall's corners. Dogs featured in almost all of those photos, but they were too recent and could not possibly have been arranged by Edward, although with magicians – even with aspiring magicians – one could never be sure... Even more canine sculptures were lining the grand staircase, as if directing Yadwiga upstairs, to the first floor dining parlour and Edward's magnificent library.

Her heart missed a couple of beats when she saw bookshelves bursting with old folios and the old Virgil's motto above the fireplace: *Hic Vivunt Vivere Digni* – "Here live those who are worthy to live." On entering Edward's study, she gasped at the sight of his life-size mannequin in a night cap and a worn dressing gown reclining in an armchair near the fireplace. In his hands, Edward was holding a long cherry-wood pipe. He loved his pipe and referred to it as "a great soother" and a "pleasant comforter."

And again – looking at the mannequin – Yadwiga couldn't help thinking how handsome he was: with his warm brown eyes, long curly hair, carefully trimmed beard and moustache, he looked avuncular and resembled an Orthodox monk, or even an abbot. "Had Edward been alive, he would have been just a bit over two hundred years old now," she thought with sadness before her attention was drawn to his favourite books on the history and philosophy of magic, prominently displayed in a glass case. One of them – "*Saducismus Triumphatus*: or, *Full and Plain Evidence Concerning Witches and Apparitions in Two Parts, the First Treating of Their Possibility, the Second of Their Real Existence* – was Yadwiga's present for his fortieth birthday. Another – *A New Light of Alchemy: An Essay upon Reason and the Nature of Spirits* – was her gift for his fiftieth!

Next to the books were two skeletons from Pompeii which he acquired after the amazing success of his novel *The Last Days of Pompeii*. It was common knowledge that this novel had been inspired by Karl Briullov's eponymous painting, a copy of which was hanging in one of the corners of his study; but no-one, apart from Yadwiga, knew that it was she who first drew Bulwer-Lytton's attention to that painting and sent that very copy to him too!

The glass case also contained Edward's death mask – another fairly irrefutable proof of his demise – and his crystal ball. Yadwiga stared at the ball unblinkingly for a minute or so until she clearly saw in it the reflection of another room's door. She went back into the corridor and immediately recognised that door. Behind it was a "Chinese" bedroom where Dickens once stayed. Yadwiga was introduced to Dickens, but didn't like him: posh, flirty and too full of himself.

It wasn't the little toy pagoda or the bronze Chinese cauldron that grabbed her attention in the bedroom. In a glass case near the window, she saw a life-size Meissen porcelain sculpture of a lap-dog resting on the carpet, with his elongated black-nosed face pointing ahead, like an arrow. Yadwiga went in the direction of that "arrow" and was soon inside Elizabeth's bedroom. With fresh flowers and an open book on the edge of the bed, it looked as if Edward's mother was still living there and had simply popped out for a moment. Behind the mantelpiece clock was an engraved inscription left by Edward: "This room long occupied by Elizabeth Bulwer-Lytton and containing the relics most associated with her memory her son trusts that her descendants will preserve unaltered – *LIBERIS VIRTUTIS EXEMPLAR* (set free by virtue of the highest order)."

After Elizabeth's death, Edward vouched publicly that her bedroom would be kept intact for generations to come. And it was. Yadwiga felt very strongly that the clue, left by her lover, must be somewhere in there – and in a moment she knew where it was! On both sides of the false door to the right of the four-poster bed were two paintings of one and the same dog – an Italian pug named Juba, and underneath one of them was a caption: "This picture is to commemorate extraordinary canine sagacity, fidelity and attachment. July 1821." Juba was obviously Elizabeth's favourite pet, yet placing two paintings of him next to each other, with only the false door separating them, was a bit over the top. Having squinted at both paintings, Yadwiga noticed that the two Jubas (or rather one and the same Juba in his two artistic incarnations) were looking at each other, as if trying to draw an observant viewer's attention to the false door that separated them. Yes, both paintings were focused on the door, as if inviting to open it, if only to make sure that, unlike the entry to the magic passageway inside the Covent Garden bookshop described in *Zanoni*, this one – with just a stuccoed stone wall behind it – was leading absolutely nowhere!

Yadwiga suddenly had a very clear realisation that she had cracked the password. It was "Juba!"

On her way out of the house, she kept jubilantly repeating in her head her favourite quote from Edward's novel *Harold, the Last of the Saxons*: "It is the persons we love that make beautiful the haunts we have known. Those persons at least we shall behold again, and wherever they are – there is heaven."

Prancing along the corridors of Knebworth House, Yadwiga felt exhilarated, as if she had just seen Edward, spoken with him and he was now walking next to her, happy that she had uncovered his hidden message which might lead her to the receptacle of Koshchei's life and death and make her immortal and – who knows – possibly even young again."

At this moment, to Koshchei's annoyance, the typing stopped. A frantic scratching noise could be heard from the porch of Pegasus Cottage. The Writer – with badly concealed relief – stood up from his swivel chair and opened the door.

"Is it you, Koshchei?" he said. "There's no food for you here!"

A large and very thin ginger cat burst into the garden office and promptly climbed onto the desk hissing loudly. The Writer watched in disbelief as a black squirrel emerged from behind the tea kettle, dexterously jumped over the cat, bounced off the floor and – through the open door – dashed out into the garden. Koshchei's feline namesake chased him, but soon gave up.

* * *

Back in the leafy and quiet town street, Koshchei regained his normal looks. He was breathing heavily, but was very pleased with himself. There was no time, however, to savour his success, for one other important thing had to be done before he could fly back to London and then to the bookshop in Bloomsbury.

From the folds of his loose shroud-like cloak, he ferreted out a mobile phone and, having changed his voice, made two phone calls – one after another.

As he was doing so, the Writer, having fed his ginger cat, returned to the garden office and carried on typing:

"*Yadwiga was crossing the lawn next to Knebworth House car park towards her Dyson, when her mobile rang. It was Melissa. "I have terrible news," she said. "Lucinda is dead. Give up everything and fly to Crouch End. I will meet you in one hour inside the Broadway Clock Tower."*

A second later, Melissa's phone came to life inside the Runes bookshop. Her sister Yadwiga was on the line. "I am on my way to Crouch End," she said. "Horrible news, I am afraid: Lucinda has died. Please stop whatever you are doing and fly there immediately. I will meet you in one hour inside the Crouch End train station building!"

Melissa apologised to the customer she had been serving, locked up the shop and started her Dyson…"

In the deserted town street, Koshchei was rubbing his hands in triumph. He had sent the sisters to two places which were impossible to access: there was nothing but a tiny caretaker's tool shed inside the Clock Tower, and the small wooden side door that led to it was permanently locked. As for the Crouch End station, it had been disused since 1954 when the last Edgeware, Highgate and London Railway passenger train rattled past it.

It would take ages for Yadwiga and Melissa to get their bearings and to find each other in Crouch End, where, as writer Stephen King once observed, in his short horror story *Crouch End*, "strange things still happen from time to time, and people have been known to lose their way." To be on the safe side, Koshchei decided he would also ask his old acquaintance, a Crouch End–based spriggan, to keep an eye on the sisters and let him know when they were about to leave the area. Spriggans are devious, nasty goat-like Cornish folklore creatures — who like to kidnap children, bring storms and make everyone's lives difficult. Koshchei's Crouch End contact was no different. He lived under a footbridge of the disused railway and spent his time scaring joggers and dog walkers in Parkland Walk with high-pitched bleats and squeaky cackles…

Now Koshchei had all the time in world to quietly examine the magic passageway inside Melissa's shop. And he had the password too!

Having stretched his hands above his head, rudder-like, he jumped up in the air, made his body horizontal and whooshed off towards London.

* * *

"Bah, bah, ah, ah, ah
   Oola, Oola, ooh,la,la…"

"I want your floss" - the latest hit by Satzuma, an up-and-coming British rock star, was blasting from Olga's brand-new pink iPod, which Sergei bought her on completing a major roofing job. Four teenage girls were twitching and jumping for all they were worth to the song's ear-drum-bursting rhythm.

"I want your floss, I want your gloss.

But I don't feel like carrying your cross!"

The lyrics were largely meaningless, but that did not worry the dancers in the least. They were happy to get away from it all – from school, from controlling parents, from siblings – big and small. In short, they were "chilling out"!

The main purpose of their gathering at 125, Woodville Avenue, however, was not partying, but rehearsing. Yes, all four of them were members of their school's all-girl "Lady Yaga" rock band. The band was gaining popularity, and Olga herself had written lyrics for its theme tune:

"We are "Lady Yaga" lasses,

With tattoos on our … arms!

Making racket after classes

With guitars, keyboard and drums.

We are not just cool, but cold,

Loud, talented and sweet,

Living not in a U-boat,

But in huts on chicken's feet!"

A long meaningful pause after "With tattoos on our…" in the second verse never failed to extract laughter from both the performers and the audience (if any), but Olga had to explain to the other girls the significance of the last line, of which Granny Yadwiga, incidentally, very much approved.

The school's gym, where "Lady Yaga" would normally practise, was the venue of some junior table-tennis competition that afternoon, so they were left to look for an alternative place for their rehearsal. Olga suggested her house, having recalled that both her parents were at work and were not supposed to return until much later in the evening, Granny Yadwiga was again visiting her sister, and her brother Danya had his taekwondo class.

"My old folks and Hobbit are out, so we could rehearse in peace," she assured her friends.

Yet, on finding themselves inside the empty house, the girls put away their instruments and turned on the iPod. Olga made sure the volume was on the max to muffle the strange buzzing noises which could periodically be heard from the neglected and weed-riddled backyard of their neighbours.

"Girls, I adore Satzuma!" Molly, who played the bass guitar, shouted when the song came to an end.

"Yes, she is so cool!" agreed Sian, the drummer. "You haven't got anything else by her, Olga?"

"I have a terrific Satzuma video clip which I downloaded from YouTube. We can dance to that!"

Olga switched on her laptop, found the clip and clicked on the "play" arrow. The girls flocked around her and for a minute or so stayed motionless, as if mesmerised by Satzuma's eccentric and ever-so-skimpy orange-tinted attire, her elaborate twitches and all those back-up girls – or were they all multiples of Satzuma herself? – rising from oversized toothbrush holders and soap boxes, which had the words "Floss" and "Gloss" written on them, one after another. Soon all the "Lady Yaga" band members were dancing again…

They did not immediately notice a thin and pale-faced lady dressed in a worn-out shroud floating up and down in the middle of the room and waving her hands, as if dancing too. The lady was indeed not easy to notice, simply because she was almost transparent and all but blended with the lounge room's faded wallpaper and its bulky Victorian furniture. It was Olga who spotted her first, but only after she went straight through her…

"A-a-a!" she screamed at the top of her lungs. "A ghost! A ghost!"

She ran towards the locked balcony door and began pulling the handle frantically.

Olga's band mates stopped dancing and were now screaming too. Unlike Olga, they were so scared they were unable to move, as if their legs, which only a second ago were twitching, twisting and doing pirouettes, were now glued to the floor.

The girls' screams seemed to have no effect whatsoever on Pani Czerniowiecka (and it was her of course!), who kept levitating above the floor to the accompaniment of the music with a truly dead-pan expression on her pale, semi-translucent face.

Having decided that the ghost had no immediate plans to hurt her and her friends, Olga finally gained enough courage to step away from the balcony door and switch off the iPod.

The ensuing silence was so abrupt it made the girls' teeth ache.

Pani Czerniowiecka stopped dancing and side-stepped to the middle of the vast lounge room where she stood bouncing on the spot ever so slightly.

"Why are you staring at me?" she said to the girls flatly. "Haven't you ever seen a *mamuna*?"

There was no aggression in her quiet, semi-audible voice which seemed to lack any kind of intonation.

The girls kept looking at her with awe and did not respond.

"You could at least say hello to your landlady," continued Pani Czerniowiecka. "Here I am: home after a whole year inside a coffin, and what kind of welcome do I get? Where is Yadwiga?"

"She... she... is away with her sister," Olga muttered from the corner. "Would you... would you care for a cup of tea?"

She had already come to grips with that admirable English custom to resort to a nice cuppa when faced with an impasse or simply unsure what to do next.

"Thank you, dear, but I don't drink or eat. Not when straight from the grave, you know... Have to re-adjust myself to being alive little by little."

That was too much for Olga's friends to take. They squealed and, having picked up their cases with musical instruments, dashed towards the corridor nearly bumping into Sergei, who had just come in and was standing in the doorway clutching his toolkit.

"Lots of noise but no fighting!" he exclaimed using a popular Slavonian saying. "What's going on here?"

"Daddy," Olga said timidly. "Please meet my friends from school and... and also our landlady who is just back from the grave."

Chapter Fourteen

In which Yadwiga bumps into Bulgakov and his new friends in a Crouch End café, the Sablins confront Pani Czerniowiecka and Koshchei tries to use the stolen password

I T DIDN'T take Yadwiga long to establish that the Crouch End railway station was no more. Having made a couple of circles above the suburb, to which she was guided by her Dyson's embedded GPS, and still airborne, she was unable to spot any sign of a station or of a railway track. In one place, she could clearly see the remains of a platform with a footbridge in the middle of what looked like a small forest or a park. But the platform, overgrown with the previous year's brownish grass, looked lifeless and abandoned. Luckily, her GPS had an additional function, activated not by a normal switch, but by a red "witch on" button. When in "witched on" – as opposed to just "switched on" – mode, the device could take you to destinations which no longer existed in Todayland.

Having put her Dyson in a cruise control regime, Yadwiga typed "Crouch End Railway Station" on a small liquid-crystal monitor screen and pressed the "witch on" button. The flying vacuum cleaner froze for one quick moment before diving down. Very soon it landed in a garden on the corner of Crouch Hill and Tregaron Avenue, next to the former station building which now housed just a small café.

Despite being clearly out of use, the station building, with its Victorian gables and slanting roof, was still recognisable. Having parked and padlocked her Dyson, Yadwiga headed towards the café wondering why, by Perun, Melissa had chosen to meet inside a station which didn't exist anymore. Knowing the perilous effect direct questions had on her life span, she was careful not to come up with them even in her thoughts. On the other hand, it was pleasing to realise that Koshchei's life and death were now firmly in her hands and that, with the password uncovered, getting hold of the egg was just a matter of hours away. She was increasingly tempted to stop fretting about it all. Soon, very soon, she would be able to ask and answer any number of questions without adding wrinkles to her skin.

It was past breakfast time and not quite the time for lunch, so the café was empty. A sleepy waitress in a blue apron materialised from behind the till. Yadwiga ordered a cup of camomile tea. She was herself twenty minutes late, and the fact that Melissa, who had always been punctual, was not there yet worried her. She took out her mobile and dialled both her sister's numbers: one that Melissa used for work and an unlisted private one, preceded by a special personalised "witch code": 4539111 – the numerological equivalent of Melissa's name, where 4 stood for "M", 5 for "E", 3 for "L", 9 for "I" and 1 for "S" and "A".

But both Melissa's phones were firmly switched off. And "witched off" too.

"No cats, sorry!" Yadwiga was so lost in thought and in worry that the waitress's angry yell caught her by surprise and made her wince. She looked back and saw Bulgakov standing in the doorway on his hind legs with a bundle of books under his armpit. Behind him, there were three strangers: a policeman in a helmet, a tall middle-aged gentleman in a rumpled corduroy suit and a teenage boy with an old and bulky Pentax camera hanging from a strap across his chest.

"It's OK, love," the policeman said to the waitress quietly. "The cat is with me."

All four of them came up to Yadwiga's table, pulled out chairs and, without asking for a permission or even saying "hi," sat down.

"Bulgakov, please explain how on earth you got here!" Yadwiga demanded in shock, yet still being careful not to sound interrogative.

"No worries, I will explain everything in a moment," the Cat answered. "But before I do that, please meet my new friends: PC

Robert Farnham, Mr Leornard Freeman, or simply Lonnie – an American lawyer, and Matthew King."

"Gentlemen," he then said to the men. "It is my absolute pleasure to introduce to you my Slavonian owner and friend Miss Yadwiga Yaghina, better known as Baba Yaga."

All three of them stood up and took turns to shake Yadwiga's small wrinkled hand.

From behind the till there came a muffled bang: it was the waitress, who fainted at the sight and sound of a talking cat.

"I am delighted to meet you all, gentlemen," said Yadwiga. "But before we proceed any further, this cat owes me an explanation. The truth is that not only is he not supposed to be here, but also that simply walking into this café as he did a minute ago should be a total and utter impossibility due to certain dimensional parameters over which he has no control!"

"I know a couple of things about dimensions, ma'am," said the policeman. "My senior colleague PC Ted Vetter was right when he told me that Crouch End was the place where the borders between our world and other realities, or dimensions, if you wish, were at their thinnest."

"You bet! I felt it on my own goddam skin! And my whole goddam body too!" intervened the lawyer. He had a thick American accent.

"Bulgakov, tell me what's going on!" Yadwiga demanded again.

"Well, these two gentlemen have partially explained it all already," shrugged the Cat. "The full answer, however, is here!" He put two out of the three books he had been holding onto the table and pushed them towards Yadwiga.

"As you might have already guessed, these three men are not creatures of Today," continued Bulgakov. "Nor do they fully belong in Yesterdayland."

"I want to know where they are from then!" Yadwiga exclaimed.

"The respected lawyer is from 'Crouch End', a horror story by Steven King, and the young man is from 'Killer Camera' by Anthony Horowitz!".

The Cat interrupted his monologue to address the boy, "Matthew, will you be so kind as to stop fiddling with your camera this very moment? Or do you want us all dead?"

"Sorry!" said the boy and obediently put both his hands on the table.

"In the story, he buys this old camera at a car boot sale in Crouch End as a present for his dad, but soon discovers that anything or anyone he takes a photo of gets promptly destroyed or dies," explained Bulgakov. "As for Stephen King's novella, it is all about the sinister side of Crouch End which happens to act as a natural portal to other, mostly horrific, dimensions into which both Mr Farnham, a local copper, and Mr Freeman, an American lawyer who had moved to London with his wife and came to Crouch End to visit his potential employer, eventually disappear."

"This is all very nice," said Yadwiga. "Sorry, gentlemen, I don't mean to say that what's happened to each of you is in any way nice, it is of course entirely awful... but it still doesn't explain your presence here."

"I am coming to that," said the Cat. "As you know, bored and lonely in my forced Yesterdayland exile, I have learned to read books not just from the past, but also from the future – including those that haven't been published or even written yet. But I have done more than that: I have found a way of entering the world of books – yet another dimension where fiction and literature come to life. It is called Bookland, and I had always felt it should have existed somewhere. Why not? After all, both you, Yadwiga, and I are creatures of fiction, products of the Writer's imagination. And we do exist, there's little doubt about it. My rationale was that countless other fictional characters, like ourselves, must be dwelling somewhere too. That was how I discovered Bookland and for many long years had been looking for a way to access it. When you told me about

Lucinda's sightings in Crouch End, I got some new literature about the place, including the two books in front of you, on top of this one which I had lent to you before."

He showed Yadwiga the third book he had been carrying – *The Quantity Theory of Insanity* by Will Self.

"As you may remember, this collection opens with a story, 'The North London Book of the Dead', about the main character's mother who ended up living in Crouch End after she died. A number of writers have hinted at the area's spooky nature. On top of this, as you may have heard, the Highgate Vampire himself used to have a temporary abode in a neo-Gothic mansion not far from here, in Avenue Road… I decided to investigate further and discovered that, due to the flimsiest imaginable veils between different dimensions running through Crouch End, here I could easily access Today from Yesterdayland without having to resort to the Ely Place portal. I also found out that it was from here, from this very former station building, that we could enter the domain of literature. In fact, believe it or not, the entrance to this café doubles as London's only gateway to Bookland. The Bookland border, by the way, is clearly marked at the end of Northwood Road, Archway, with an old 'Warning to Trespassers' sign, green with age, of which only one half is still visible from Today – you can go and check it out yourself, Yadwiga, it says '…ng to Trespassers' – you can't miss it!"

"And have you ever taken the trouble of reading the last two lines of that goddam sign?" interrupted Leonard Freeman. "Go and have a good look, but don't forget your goddam glasses. These lines go: 'Trespassers are… or imprisonment for every…' with the 'y' in 'every' hardly visible at all! So, in actual fact, it threatens the trespassers with 'imprisonment for ever' – and that was exactly what I got: stuck in that goddam black hole until the end of my life!"

He paused to regain his breath and continued on a calmer note: "What I mean is that the sign marks the border with not just Bookland, but other dimensions stemming from it, some of which are very, very sinister and which – once sucked in – you cannot escape!"

"This is exactly right!" agreed Bulgakov. "That border runs along the disused railway track, or Parkland Walk, as they call it now, all the way to Finsbury Park. On its way, it has multiple junctions and intersections with Yesterdayland and other dimensions, mentioned here by Mr Freeman, to the extent that it is sometimes hard to distinguish between them. In many instances, it is hard to establish where Yesterdayland ends and Bookland begins, because most fiction, with the exception of futuristic and utopian novels, is firmly based in the past!"

Bulgakov looked at Yadwiga triumphantly with his piercing deep green eyes and continued:

"Since this discovery, my life in Yesterdayland had become much richer. Every morning I would travel to Today's Crouch End and, via it, to Bookland to catch up with other feline literary characters: the Brothers Grimm's Puss in Boots; Pushkin's Learned Cat from *Ruslan and Ludmila*; the Cheshire Cat from *Alice in Wonderland*; Kipling's Cat That Walked by Himself; Behemoth, the walking, talking and vodka-drinking cat from *The Master and Margarita* by my namesake, Mikhail Bulgakov, and so on. And though Pushkin's Learned Cat and I are true soul mates and have a lot in common, as I do with the Cheshire Cat whose elusive smile and iron logic I have come to admire, I find Behemoth rather uncouth, almost like Snake Horinich, and his habits – heavy drinking and swearing like a cobbler – outright disgusting. Not my type of a cat at all, despite claiming to be my brother. Or take Macavity, T.S. Eliot's Mystery Cat, alias Hidden Paw – a felon, as opposed to a feline, with a long criminal record! But no world, not even Bookland, is perfect."

"You still haven't explained how you found me here," persisted Yadwiga.

"By pure coincidence! I spotted you on my way to Bookland this morning and thought you might like to meet my new fictional friends, so I was able to bring them to Today briefly with the help of those books I am carrying. But now, Yadwiga, I would be very tempted to ask *you* a question too. Of course, I am not going to do so knowing about Koshchei's curse..."

Yadwiga was suddenly reminded of Koshchei and thought she should get to the egg soon, on finding out what happened to Lucinda, for Koshchei, she knew, would stop at nothing to prevent her from doing so.

"I know, Bulgakov, what you want to ask me, and thanks for being tactful for a change," she said to the Cat. "The matter that had brought me to Crouch End is rather gruesome. Or appears to be. I had a phone call from Melissa telling me that Lucinda had died. On reflection, I find it strange. Firstly, because Lucinda, just like Melissa, should be immortal. On the other hand, I used to be immortal as well... You never know with Koshchei. He could have easily taken away Lucinda's immortality too by making her look and feel her true age, over a thousand years old – his well-known nasty trick whereby a *ved'ma*, having suddenly lost her immortality, literally expires in front of one's eyes. The other thing that worries me is the absence of Melissa, who was supposed to be here over an hour ago"

At that very moment, Yadwiga's mobile rang. It was Melissa, who had just exited the Clock Tower, where she had been patiently waiting for Yadwiga crouched inside a broom cupboard.

"If I were to write a story about sitting there in the dark and feeling trapped, I would call it 'Crouched in Crouch End'!" she said sarcastically.

The sisters realised they had been conned, and Yadwiga told Melissa to make her way to the café as fast as she could.

"It must have been Koshchei!" Melissa exclaimed the moment she burst in through the door five minutes later.

"It might have well been him, but even so we cannot leave here without making sure Lucinda is alive," Yadwiga replied.

"I have an idea!" PC Farnham said suddenly. "I've been policing this area for long enough to know that whenever someone dies in Bookland's Crouch End, his or her name immediately gets entered in

The North London Book of the Dead from Will Self's short story, so we simply have to look your sister's name up, and if it's not there, that would mean she is alive!"

"But if she did die, it must have happened very recently, and there might not have been enough time for her name to appear in the book," objected Yadwiga.

"Look, ma'am, I am a police officer, and I am telling you that the name of a dead person appears in the book the moment he or she passes on. Trust me!"

"Very well, but how can we find the book?" said Melisssa and, turning to Yadwiga, hastened to add: "Sorry, sister, this question was not addressed to you directly, so should have no immediate effect on your life span."

"This should be easy!" exclaimed Bulgakov. "We all cross into Bookland and find the house where the protagonist's dead mother lives – there's an exact address in Will Self's story! I can then sneak in through the door or a window, get the book and take it out for us to look at. Or else we ask Matthew to aim his killer camera at the house and take a photo. As the house collapses, we'll all be able to get in and take a good look at the book!"

"Yes, I will do that!" Matthew King agreed readily and grasped his horrible camera, mockingly aiming it at the waitress, who had just come back to her senses and was towering above Yadwiga with a cup of lukewarm camomile tea.

"Put that damn thing down!" Leonard Freeman yelled at the boy. He then turned towards Bulgakov.

"I may not live in a real world any longer, but I am still a damn good lawyer!" he said. "What you have suggested is called aggravated break-in and intentional destruction of private property – a very serious crime by all standards."

"But we are talking about a dead person," Bulgakov tried to protest. "What kind of private property can a deceased old woman claim to own?"

"In the dimension where I happen to live now, it makes little difference if you are alive or dead!" the lawyer replied and added sombrely: "Forgot who it was who said that for a writer death is just a career change…"

"OK, OK, we'll knock on the door and politely ask the dead mother to show us the book then."

"How do you know she has it?" asked Melissa, and again threw a furtive look at Yadwiga to make sure that the question did not age her.

"This is how," replied Bulgakov, opening Will Self's *The Quantity Theory of Insanity*:

There were phone directories stacked under the table – phone directories and something else, phone-directory-shaped, that wasn't a phone directory. I bent down and pulled it out by its spine. It was a phone directory. North London Book of the Dead, ran the title; and then underneath: A–Z. The cover was the usual yellow flimsy card and there was also the usual vaguely arty line drawing – in this instance of Kensal Green Cemetery…

"By reading this to you, I have just made sure that *The North London Book of the Dead* is still there, for this is how it works in Bookland: as long as the story is being read even by one person, the realities it describes get into place!"

"Let's go then! We mustn't waste any more time!" Yadwiga said authoritatively. She stood up from the table with the untouched cup of camomile tea on it and headed for the exit.

"Wait," said PC Robert Farnham. "It is our domain we are going to, after all, so let me lead the way."

* * *

"It is very kind of you, Miss Czerniowiecka, but I don't think we can accept your hospitality any longer," Irina said firmly.

It was an extended meeting of the Sablin family, to which Pani Czerniowiecka was invited in her role as the owner of the house at

125, Woodville Avenue. The meeting was being held in the evening of the same day on which the absentee-landlady-cum-demon made her appearance at the Lady Yaga band members' dance party. Irina and Danya came back home immediately after Sergei, just in time to see the quickly receding backs of Olga's classmates running away from the house at record speeds. Irina was no less shocked than the girls when she got her first glimpse of Pani Czerniowiecka in all her semi-transparency floating above the floor in the lounge room, which suddenly felt stale and chilly, like a freshly dug out grave. However, being the most composed and strong-willed of the Sablins, she was doing her best not to show it.

As for Danya, who knew about their landlady's true nature from Granny Yadwiga, yet was still unable to overcome his fear, he was the only family member who was not particularly surprised. Trying not to look at the landlady, he just said politely: "Good afternoon, Miss Czerniowiecka! Welcome back home!" before retiring to his room with skull and crossbones above the hand-written sign (aimed primarily at Olga): 'Leave Hope Ye Who Enter Here!' There he sat in the dark for a couple of minutes wondering what sort of presents he was going to get for his eleventh birthday the following morning.

"It is very nice to meet you at last," Irina volunteered to shake hands with Pani Czerniowiecka and immediately regretted it: the landlady's hand was soft, wet and cold like a jellyfish. She then suggested they get together in the lounge in one hour and discuss the new situation inside the house over a cup of tea.

"Miss Czerniowiecka doesn't eat or drink," Olga whispered into her mother's ear. Her remark was overheard by Pani Czerniowiecka who said: "The young lady is right: I can't consume any food or drink during the first two or three months of being alive. My body takes time to readjust after a year of being dead and resting inside a coffin."

That explanation did little to cheer up Irina and Sergei, and by the time they all sat down around a massive oak table near the bay window overlooking the garden, they had made their decision.

Not to distract the Sablins with her body's involuntary fluctuations and to remain stationary during the conversation, Pani Czerniowiecka, who had lost almost all her weight while in the grave, had to strap herself to a chair. Sergei and Irina were sipping their cups of tea, while Olga and Danya kept kicking each other jokingly under the table.

Sergei coughed out gently, asking for attention. He felt as if he were about to address a trade union meeting at his factory in Slavonia.

"Dear Miss Czerniowiecka," he said solemnly. "First of all, allow me on behalf of all the family to thank you for having harboured us in your house for several difficult months. I am sure Yadwiga would have added her thanks to mine, had she been around, but she is still with her sister in Bloomsbury and is not expected back until tomorrow"

He paused and was immediately interrupted by Pani Czerniowiecka's flat and toneless voice:

"It was my pleasure to have you and still is. Yadwiga told me a lot of good things about you all when she visited me briefly at the cemetery last January. I know that my looks and… er… manners may seem unusual to you, even scary. But I want to stress that inside I am a kind and harmless creature, both when alive and when… when temporarily dead. When dead, I am also extremely quiet, as you might have guessed, ha-ha-ha…"

Pani Czerniowiecka was speaking with her one and only facial expression: eyes half-shut and not making eye contact with anyone or anything except for the floor. Her dry laughter resembled the croaking of a frog in a swamp of an evening.

"Lots of nasty rumours have been circulating about *mamunas*," she carried on. "And indeed, some of us can be really wicked: kidnapping children, making horrible noises at night, overeating massively when alive. But believe me, I am different: I like people and hate being on my own when undead, so you are welcome to remain my guests for as long as you wish, and I promise to stay out of your way as much as I can…"

It was now Irina's turn to intervene.

"Very kind of you, ma'am, but unfortunately we cannot stay here any longer. The reason is simple: we want to travel, to see the world, to visit Scotland, Italy, America, and Australia. As you know, we weren't allowed to travel at all while in Slavonia, and it is extremely important for the children to broaden their horizons."

"I want to stay here!" said Danya. "I like my school and my martial arts class and do not feel like travelling!"

"I also enjoy my school and our band!" echoed Olga.

"We are only going to travel for one year," said Irina. "Then we'll come back – and if Pani Czerniowiecka still wants to have us, will stay here again…"

"But I won't be home then!" said Pani Czerniowiecka with a sudden tinge of emotion in her voice. "In one year, I'll have to return to the blasted cemetery, where I'll have to spend another year with no-one but the Highgate Vampire for company. In certain ways, he is not unattractive: seven foot tall, and with a touch of celebrity too, but despite being a devoted *Observer* reader, he is not much fun to be with. And even he often takes a ley line to Crouch End with his coffin and leaves me entirely on my own. There's nothing I can do about it though: this is how we *mamunas* work, and I cannot change it."

"Well, we may come a bit earlier to spend some time with you then," Irina lied.

"But travelling is expensive. Where are you going to get the money?"

"Sergei and I have both been working for a while, so we've saved some," Irina lied again. "Besides, we are going to keep working wherever we are and the kids will keep attending schools."

"And what about Yadwiga? Is she coming with you too?"

"We'll ask her when she returns, but I don't see why not."

"Well, good luck to you then. When are you leaving?"

"Tomorrow. When Yadwiga comes back. So we'd better start packing now."

The Sablins stood up from the table and went to their rooms. Irina's main worry, however, was not packing or travelling. Nor even the prospect of being homeless again. She simply could not fathom how they would spend the night under one roof with a zombie, no matter how polite and hospitable. The very thought of it made her tremble with fear for her children. And for herself and Sergei too.

Until four o'clock in the morning, Irina tossed and turned in her bed, unable to sleep and listening to every little noise inside the house. Then she suddenly remembered that today was Danya's eleventh birthday and that she hadn't bought him a present yet!

* * *

In the semi-dark basement of the Runes bookshop, Koshchei was staring at the wall. Trying to prolong the moment of his triumph, he was not in a hurry to utter the magic password. He had just heard back from the Crouch End spriggan that Yadwiga and Melissa had left the café inside the former railway station building and, having passed underneath the footbridge, were moving towards Crouch End Broadway. One slightly worrying aspect of the spriggan's report was that the sisters were being accompanied, among others, by a uniformed policeman and a young man with a huge camera – most likely a journalist.

Yet Koshchei decided to put all his worries aside. In a matter of minutes, he would recover the egg with his life and take it elsewhere, to a place where no-one would ever be able to find it, simply because no-one, not even writers – Victorian or modern – would have a clue as to its whereabouts. No-one would, except for himself. And that would be the ultimate guarantee of his everlasting immortality.

"Everlasting immortality" was, of course, a repetition, a tautology, but Koshchei allowed himself the pleasure of repeating it silently, savouring it in his mind like a person with a sweet tooth sucks on a particularly yummy "long-playing" lolly ever so slowly.

"Well, it's time to get it done!" he finally decided. Facing the wall, he – loudly and clearly – uttered "Ju-ba! Ju-ba!"

To him, the magic word was meant to sound like the name of his favourite "Star Wars" character, Jabba the Hutt – a fat slug-like alien and an intergalactic villain. At least, that was how he thought he had to pronounce it: "Jar-ba!"

The wall remained still. Not only it was refusing to open up to reveal a hidden passage, but it didn't budge a single inch and stood motionless as a rock.

Koshchei repeated the word again, then again and again, yelled it out at the top of his lungs, and whispered it semi-audibly – nothing!

After half an hour of this strenuous phonetic exercise his lips and palate were hurting, and drops of cold sweat were running down his forehead.

The password did not work!

"Bloody Writer – he cheated me! I am going to turn him to a marble paperweight, like the one I saw on his desk – no – better, to a piece of dead cold concrete, like this stupid wall!" he was thinking.

It was useless to carry on.

Bent under the impact of yet another defeating blow, Koshchei trundled out of the shop into a Bloomsbury street and found himself in the middle of a cheerful and multi-lingual late afternoon crowd. Baba Yaga's invisible Black Horseman had just completed his evening ride. It was getting dark.

Chapter Fifteen

In which Yadwiga and her friends continue their search for Lucinda, while Koshchei gets hold of the egg, but not for long

THEY plodded along the Broadway, past the Clock Tower, inside which Melissa had been vainly waiting for Yadwiga only minutes before, and turned right into Tottenham Lane. Bulgakov, with a copy of the *London A to Z* under one paw and Will Self's book under the other, was leading the way. Late afternoon pedestrians were busily rushing past, and none of them seemed to be surprised by the sight of a large black cat walking on his hind legs and carrying an *A to Z*, which he consulted every now and then. One could be led to believe that, for some inexplicable reason, they were unable to see either the cat or any of his companions, as if the latter didn't actually exist in their mundane Crouch End reality – an assumption which wouldn't have been too far from the truth.

Rosemount Avenue was one of those hilltop streets in suburban London where the camber of the road is viciously arched like the back of a macadamised whale. The houses are high-gabled Victorian, tiled in red and with masonry that looks as if it was sculpted out of solid snot...

Bulgakov closed *The Quantity Theory of Insanity* and looked around. They had just turned left into a side street which corresponded precisely to Will Self's description. Only, of course, it was not called Rosemount Avenue: according to Today's *London A to Z*, there was no street with that name either in Crouch End or in the whole of Greater London, and they didn't have a copy of the *Bookland London A to Z* with them. For all Bulgakov knew, such an *A to Z* had not been published yet and was not supposed to come out in the future either. However, he was familiar enough with the creative process to realise that the author of *The Quantity Theory of Insanity* was likely to change the real street name for his story, but when doing so had probably gone for something that sounded similar. The hilly winding lane they stood on now was called Rosewood Gardens. Having altered the name of the street, the novelist could safely preserve the original house number without fearing a legal claim from disgruntled or plain greedy occupiers.

"The basement of No. 24 looked rather poky from the street; I couldn't see the windows without going down into the basement area…" Bulgakov kept reading aloud – not so much for the benefit of his companions as to further evoke and bring to life the elusive Bookland reality.

They walked up the street to house number 24B, where "B" obviously stood for "basement." It was getting dark, but in the light of a street lantern they were able to see that the windows of the basement flat were barred and boarded up. The small entrance door, with cobwebs in its corners and rust on its hinges, was locked and covered with a thick layer of dust, as if no-one had come in or out of it for a long time. An equally dusty plastic wheelie rubbish bin in front of the door appeared empty, untouched and "un-wheeled" for many months. In short, it was an ideal dead person's abode!

"Let me take a quick flash photo of it!" suggested Matthew King.

"Don't you dare!" snapped PC Farnham. Having asked everybody in the group to move ten yards up the street and away from the property, he resolutely walked down the steps, moved away the rubbish bin and, having knocked at the door three times, said peremptorily: "Police! Open up!"

The door was answered almost immediately by a frail elderly lady who looked considerably older than Yadwiga. She was dressed in a extremely loose shroud-like nightgown, and plastic hair-curlers could be seen under the towel wrapped around her head.

"Terribly sorry for the disturbance, ma'am. I am PC Farnham from the Crouch End police station in Tottenham Lane. Just a routine enquiry, if you please. Do you happen to be in possession of a phone directory called *The North London Book of the Dead*? I have to consult it urgently for operational reasons which I am not at liberty to disclose."

"Sorry, officer, I can't invite you inside," the old woman said apologetically. "I am expecting my son for tea any minute, and I am not quite ready, as you can see... Of course, I've got the directory: every dead household does! I'll bring the book out for you gladly, if you wait here a second..."

From the street, Yadwiga was squinting at the rectangle of pale yellow light behind the open door, but was unable to discern anything. She thought she could also feel a slight chill reaching her from the basement flat, but that was probably just an illusion.

The dead lady re-emerged with a thick, bulky yellow paperback and handed it over to the policeman.

"Many thanks, ma'am! I will return it to you in five minutes."

"What's your missing sister's full name?" he asked Yadwiga and Melissa when, back in Rosewood Gardens, they all huddled together under a lantern.

"Lucinda Yaghina," they replied. For once Yadwiga was prepared to ignore a new wrinkle on her face – the result of the policeman's question.

PC Farnham leafed through the book mumbling to himself as he did so: "Yalden... Yarrell...Yates... Yeatman..."

"Nope!" he said at last. "Your sister is not there!"

"Thank Perun!" Yadwiga exclaimed happily.

"And also, thank Svarog, Veles, Hors, Stribog and Dazhdbog!" added Melissa, bringing in some other Slavic gods: the supreme one, the god of cattle-breeders, the god of sunshine, the god of wind and the god of light – in that order – as if inviting them all to join Perun, god of thunder and lightning, in celebration of Lucinda's ongoing life.

"Before you start celebrating, I have to warn you that there still is one small possibility that the lady may be dead," PC Farnham said to the sisters. "Well, this doesn't happen often, but since a kind of housing crisis began among the dead of this area and of the whole of London in 1854, the deceased have occasionally been very quickly transported by the specially constructed Necropolis Railway to Brookwood in Surrey, where they had, and still have, a bit more space. Particularly if the deceased had no immediate family at hand to accommodate him or her, in which case his or her name would actually appear in *The Surrey Book of the Dead*, for it is there that this particular dead person would be expected to reside."

"That's ridiculous!" interrupted Yadwiga. "From what I know the Necropolis Railway has been out of use for over seventy years!"

"Not in Bookland, ma'am, not in Bookland, where it is still functioning and has regular services between Waterloo and Brookwood Cemetery, in its own time slot, of course. It is part of BDRN – Bookland Dead Railways Network which, incidentally, incorporates the Edgeware, Highgate and London Railway that used to run – and in Bookland still does – via Crouch End. So if you were to travel to Brookwood, you could catch a dead train straight here, then change at Westminster Bridge Road."

Yadwiga and Melissa were shocked.

"Well, I guess we need to go there," Yadwiga said after a pause. "Just to be absolutely sure that Lucinda is still alive."

"You are right, sister," agreed Melissa. "Giving up now would mean continuing uncertainty about Lucinda's fate."

"But where can we get a copy of *The Surrey Book of the Dead*?" Melissa asked PC Farnham. "And would you or Mr Freeman be able to accompany us and assist in our search?"

"As for the book, there shouldn't be a problem getting hold of it when in Brookwood," replied the policeman. "One of our DCs saw a copy at the former South Station Chapel which is now known as St Edward's Monastery and is home to four very helpful Orthodox monks. If not, you could try the cemetery office next to the main road. As for us, we cannot accompany you any further, I am afraid. As our new friend Bulgakov will confirm, we can only exist in the Bookland dimension of Crouch End. Until and unless another book, which places us somewhere else, gets written, which is highly unlikely."

"I have to agree with PC Farnham," Bulgakov said with a sigh. "So far I haven't been able to trace – in the past or in the future – any other work of fiction where our three new friends feature again."

"Well, goodbye then and thanks for all your help! We must rush!" said Yadwiga. Having shaken hands with PC Farnham, Leonard Freeman and Matthew King (who brazenly suggested taking a photo of all of them in memory of their meeting, an idea that was vigorously rejected by everyone), Yadwiga, Melissa and Bulgakov hurried back to the station.

Crouch End was immersed in darkness.

"Hopefully, they still run some dead-of-the-night dead train services here," Yadwiga thought, and a touch of a rueful smile lit up her heavily wrinkled parchment-like face.

* * *

With his head down, Koshchei – feeling duped and defeated – was aimlessly wandering the crowded streets of Bloomsbury. Next to Russell Square Tube Station, he was approached by a curiously dressed young man. It was a chilly evening in mid-May, yet the man was wearing khaki shorts which ended right below his knees and a wide-brimmed felt hat, known in Australia as an akubra.

"G'day, *mite*!" he greeted Koshchei vociferously and tried to pat him on the shoulder – the latter had to duck to avoid the familiarity. "Ya don't have a piece of *piper* and a *pin*, do ya, *mite*? I want to write down this Sheila girl's email?" he pointed at a smiling young woman behind him.

Koshchei stared straight in the man's face with his fiery yellow eyes.

"I don't have any pipers and if you try to call me 'mite' again, I'll make sure you find yourself back down under and spread all over Ayers Rock, like vegemite on a piece of toast, before you can say 'Sheila' again!" he hissed out.

The man was visibly taken aback by such a ferocious response from the old frail-looking bloke and was about to reply in kind when his female companion covered his mouth with her hand.

"Leave this old loser alone, *Jyson!*" she said. "Can't you see he is starkers, walking around London in a bloody dressing gown and standing out in the crowd like a brick dunny in the desert? He will cark and, dead as mutton chops, will be pushing daisies *anywhy* soon!"

The Australian couple walked away hand in hand, but Koshchei was still fuming.

"Piper... pin... mite... what a dipstick!" he was thinking angrily, having realised he did come very close to throwing the impertinent tourist back to Australia and indeed turning him into a red boulder on top of that famous Aussie rock. "But what the hell did he mean by 'a piece of piper' and why did he call me 'mite' when, in actual fact, I am far from a midget??"

He stopped and looked up at the dark starry sky.

"And his horrible girlfriend, or whoever she was..." he kept fuming. "Did she mean to say I was going to die soon? 'Pushing daisies,' my foot! She had no idea I am deathless!"

He suddenly remembered his fiasco to get hold of the egg and bit his wrist in frustration.

"Damn! The woman could be right, and, if Yadwiga gets to the egg first, I could indeed bite the dust any time soon! Stupid, stupid Sheila and her blockhead of a boyfriend, what did she call him – 'Jyson?' What a strange name – or maybe she meant 'Jason'? Of course she did! They are Australians, after all, and had very strong Aussie accents..."

The realisation hit him like a hammer.

"*Pipe*" and "*pin*" were of course "paper" and "pen" and "*mite*" was just "mate" – a friendly way of addressing a stranger! How could he forget that Australians often say "ai" instead of "ei" and "i" instead of "e"? Their peculiar way of talking through their teeth, to prevent too many flies from ending up in their mouths, as they themselves liked to say jokingly, made some words hard to recognise and some – totally incomprehensible!

At that particular moment, evening pedestrians in Russell Square could observe a tall old man in a long star-spangled mantle and a pointed hat suddenly turn around in his tracks and run back to where he had just come from – towards the British Museum. They could assume that the eccentric oldie must have left behind something important and wanted to retrieve whatever it was before it got nicked. And they would be spot on!

Within minutes, Koshchei was back inside Melissa's shop. He knew it was going to work this time, for the correct pronunciation of the password must have been *Jooba*, not *Jarba*, as his passion for "Star Wars" had led – or rather misled – him to believe. Ten minutes later, he emerged from the shop with a small parcel in his pocket. Triumph written all over his face, he stealthily looked around and, having made sure the lane was deserted and no-one saw him coming out of the locked shop, walked away quickly. He did for a moment contemplate flying back to his Hampstead Heath castle, but decided that he wanted to walk. Had he flown, most of the events that followed wouldn't have happened...

Anybody able to see what was in Koshchei's pocket (and at that particular time there was at least one person who desperately wanted to) would have been disappointed to learn that it was but an ordinary-looking oblong object wrapped in a piece of a coarse cotton fabric, similar to the one used to make sacks and sails. The object was indeed the egg which contained a needle with Koshchei's life on its top. Yet if anyone bothered to unwrap the piece of "duck" – and that is the correct name for the cloth the egg was wrapped in – he, she or it (for some mythical creatures of Bookland like *sciopods*, *panotiis* or, say, *blemmyas* are utterly genderless!) would see that the egg in question was far from ordinary. It was a work of art rather than the product of a hen's, duck's or even ostrich's body (let alone bottom!). Yes, inside the duck-covered parcel (remember: "inside an egg inside the duck!") was a richly jewelled and enamelled Imperial Fabergé Egg, one of the fifty-one made by the famous House of Fabergé between 1885 and 1917.

Yes, fifty-one and not fifty, as any dictionary or handbook of antiques asserts, for the egg in Koshchei's pocket was the fifty-first Imperial Fabergé egg, the very existence of which was known only to Peter Carl Fabergé himself (who died in 1920) and to Koshchei. It was the latter's idea to replace an ordinary hen's egg with his life inside it with a beautiful – and much harder to crack! – Fabergé one.

The history of Fabergé eggs began in 1885 with an egg in the shape of a hen, the now famous Hen Egg. Inside its exquisite mother-of-pearl shell was a piece of "yolk" made of gold; inside the yolk a miniature gold hen; and inside the hen a crown with a ruby pendant: three "surprises" in one egg! The second Imperial Egg (which, by the way, is still officially missing), called "Hen with Sapphire Pendant", was similar to the first one and contained a surprise too. It is quite obvious that the idea of the egg in which a yolk, a symbol of new life, and another hen were hidden was prompted to Peter Carl Fabergé by the story of Koshchei's own peculiar life and death arrangements ("a needle inside an egg inside the duck"), grasped from old legends and fairy tales which he had adored since childhood. When one fine day a real, flesh-and-bone (lots of bones and not too much flesh) Koshchei appeared in front of the unsuspecting jeweller and claimed copyright for the idea, Peter Carl was easily persuaded to pay him off to avoid litigation, in the best scenario, and mutilation or transformation in the worst. That was how the egg, provisionally called "Koshchei's Life and Death", was first devised and then manufactured.

The super-vital needle with Kohschei's life (and death) on its top was carefully transferred inside that richly decorated masterpiece of jewellery. While, in the course of time, Fabergé Eggs were getting more and more famous, collectable and pricey – some of them even became truly priceless – "Koshchei's Life and Death" remained unknown to experts, although it was getting harder and harder to conceal its whereabouts from the prying eyes of international moneybags and obsessive collectors. In fact, constantly hiding and re-hiding the egg became so cumbersome and confusing that at some point Koshchei himself lost track of the duck-wrapped parcel and was unsure as to its whereabouts until that very evening when he managed to recover it from the well-concealed and password-protected magic passageway in the basement of the Runes bookshop in Bloomsbury.

When Koshchei thought no-one could see him leaving the shop, he was wrong. Crispin Sneaky, the pickpocket, had been watching him closely since his sudden turnaround in Russell Square. Here it has to be said that Crispin's urge to change his life and to become a plumber, which he had experienced briefly on spotting Yadwiga in the night sky above Bloomsbury, did not last. Because of his lengthy criminal record, no employer was willing to give him a job or to send him on a training course. After a couple of weeks of futile attempts, he reverted to his old routine – targeting forgetful tourists, particularly foreigners, inside and around the British Museum.

Koshchei and his eccentric attire could not fail to attract Crispin's attention, particularly when he saw him staring at the sky while mumbling something to himself and then turning around and running back to where he had come from. The man was clearly a foreigner and most likely a bit gaga too – an ideal target. Crispin followed Koshchei all the way to the Runes and wondered how the latter entered the locked shop quite literally through the wall. He then hid in the doorway of an adjoining house until the fuddy-duddy foreign geezer in a nightgown emerged ten minutes later – again through the wall – holding a small parcel wrapped in a piece of rag. From the way the old git was clutching the parcel as if his own precious life was inside it (and, as we know, it actually was!) before carefully placing it in his pocket, Crispin concluded that it had to contain something truly valuable. The fact that the old geezer must have nicked the thingy himself from a closed shop did not bother him in the least.

Followed by Sneaky, Koshchei was again nearing Russell Square Tube Station and was so immersed in his victory that he didn't notice how Crispin caught up with him noiselessly from behind and brushed past, as if trying to push his way through the evening crowd. He even looked at his watch and clicked his tongue loudly while doing so, as if saying: "I must hurry if I want to catch that train" – an old pickpockets' trick to distract the victim and to muffle down the gentle rustling sound of a dexterous thief's hand, with two outstretched fingers, going in and out of a handbag or a pocket, all within a fraction of a second.

Unlike with Map Halliday several months earlier, this time Crispin was successful, and a moment later he was pacing away briskly, while Koshchei – beaming all over his haggard face – was entering the Tube station vestibule with nothing but his battered one century travel card in his pocket.

Chapter Sixteen

In which the sisters and the Cat travel to Brookwood

YADWIGA and Melissa, with Bulgakov in tow, walked towards the station through the dead quiet streets of night-time Crouch End, dark apart from the occasional street lamp not so much lighting up as filling up its own immediate proximity with a weak yellow ganglia, almost jelly-like and so condensed that one could almost scoop it up in handfuls and cut it into pieces.

"Not so fast!" the Cat exclaimed suddenly. The sisters stopped and looked back. Bulgakov was mincing behind them on his hind legs, with his face – as usual – buried in a book.

"Bulgakov, you will ruin your eyes if you keep reading in the dark," Yadwiga said reproachfully. "We'll then have to get you a pair of spectacles. Imagine: a cat in specs – that beats Puss in Boots any time!"

"You are forgetting, Yadwiga, that we cats can see in the dark as well, and even better, than in daylight – to the point that when I read at home, in the Hut, I sometimes switch off the lights to see the text better," replied Bulgakov. "But I have something important to tell you. Before we reach the station, we have to concretise our Bookland whereabouts..."

Melissa and Yadwiga opened their mouths to cry out something like: "We have to what?" but Bulgakov resumed speaking before they had a chance to do so.

"Wait a moment, Yadwiga. When we defeat Koshchei, you'll be able to communicate with questions, but at the moment I simply cannot let you do it. What I meant to say was that time in Bookland is subject to changes and depends on the book we are reading at the moment. Now we are still on the edges of modernity, roughly in the early 1990s when *The North London Book of the Dead* story is set, and if we were to proceed to the station in the same time slot, we wouldn't be able to find anything there, because the last train on this branch of the Edgware, Highgate and London Railway left Crouch End in 1952. Likewise, our connecting London Necropolis Railway train to Brookwood would not be running either, because the traffic on that railway came to a stop even earlier – in 1941!"

"You know, he is right!" Melissa said to Yadwiga.

"Again, before you have the chance to ask me how we will get around it, I will give you an answer," continued the Cat. "What we have to do is simply start reading a book that is set inside the time slot we require which, in our case, should be somewhere around 1900 when both railways were still going strong. Actually, 1902 would be even better, because it is during that year that the then brand-new Necropolis Railway terminal in Westminster Bridge Road was completed and opened to passengers, sorry, mourners. And I think I've got exactly what we need here!"

Bulgakov walked to the nearest street lantern and showed the sisters the book he was holding – *The Hound of the Baskervilles* by Arthur Conan Doyle.

"With all my innate dislike of dogs, I have to admit this is a marvellous book," he carried on while leafing through the pages. "For the time switch to kick in, a couple of paragraphs, read aloud and listened to, should be enough. Which bit should we choose? Maybe this one where Doctor Watson and Sir Henry Baskerville are on the train from Paddington to Devonshire?"

And Bulgakov began to read:

The journey was a swift and pleasant one... In a very few hours the brown earth had become ruddy, the brick had changed to granite, and red cows grazed in

well-hedged fields where the lush grasses and more luxuriant vegetation spoke of a
richer, if a damper, climate...

He paused to regain his breath while Yadwiga and Melissa were waiting for him to continue.

"And another paragraph, just to be sure!" he announced:

The train pulled up at a small wayside station, and we all descended. Outside, beyond the low, white fence, a wagonette with a pair of cobs was waiting. Our coming was evidently a great event, for station master and porters clustered round us to carry out our luggage...

Bulgakov closed the book, lifted his head towards the light and hissed loudly. The bulb winked and went out for a second or so. When it came back on, it was no longer a yellow electric lantern of the end of the twentieth century, but a rotunda-shaped late-Victorian gas street lamp emitting a greenish flickering light. A strong smell of horse manure was in the air, and parked cars disappeared from the road, now paved with crude cobbles instead of asphalt. A two-wheeled horse-drawn cab carrying two gentlemen in bowler hats rattled past. The cabby's seat was at the back, and he was driving the carriage over the passengers' heads.

"This must have been a growler," Bulgakov mused aloud looking at the receding carriage. "Wait, no! How could I forget? Growlers had four wheels of course, so that was your typical hansom, and look how quickly it could go!"

They soon approached the station where they boarded a totally empty Edgware, Highgate and London Railway train, dragged by a constantly puffing and whistling Wardle 2-4-0T steam locomotive. At Edgware, they changed to the newly completed Bakerloo Tube. On the way to Waterloo, they saw no other passengers except for a couple of hatless drunks in rumpled frock coats. Yet, when they got off at Waterloo station, went up the stairs and turned into Westminster Bridge Road, where the imposing new building of the Necropolis Railway terminal was located, they saw a crowd of black-clad mourners. In the sombre, eerie light of the two gas lamps above the main entrance, horse-drawn funeral corteges and hearses clattered in from the street, and while their living passengers were getting off to check in at the cream- and dark-orange-tiled office, the dead, who didn't need to check in, kept lying patiently in their coffins, waiting to be loaded onto the designated "shelves," or biers, of specially designed coffin compartments for their very last journey to Brookwood. In the meantime, the parties of mourners would sit in silence in the terminal's private waiting rooms and chapels, draped in red, from where they would take lifts or stairs to the platforms in due course, while special hydraulic elevators would raise the coffins to platform level too.

In the early twentieth century, the Brookwood Cemetery line of the London and South Western Railway was in such demand that it sometimes had to operate at night, provided the families of the deceased did not mind. More often than not, they didn't, and many even preferred sobering darkness to blazing sunlight as a more appropriate environment for their loved ones' final journeys.

As Yadwiga and Melissa had expected, a stone-faced uniformed clerk in the ticket office window, from whom they acquired their first-class mourners' tickets, did not want to allow Bulgakov onto the train and remained unperturbed by the sisters' pleas that he (Bulgakov) was the favourite pet of the deceased.

"What if I buy a coffin ticket and travel on a coffin shelf?" the Cat himself suggested to the clerk. "You never know, I may choose to be buried with my beloved dead owner. Why not? It's all up to me. As my late friend Carl Gustav Jung used to say, each of us carries his own life-form within him!"

The cashier froze in the window with his mouth agape while his white-gloved hand automatically wrote out and stamped a third-class LSWR coffin ticket for the eloquent cat.

Upstairs, Bulgakov got separated from the sisters by a glass screen between the first-and the third-class platforms. Status and class distinctions were obviously very much in force in late Victorian London, not only for the living, but also for the dead. Bulgakov, however, was not affected by the sorrowful environment or by his silent neighbours, and as the funeral train – whistling ruefully – was chugging along the tracks towards Surrey, he had a great time lying on his back on a coffin shelf as if it were the sleeping bench of his favourite warm stove inside the Hut on chicken feet, and – in pitch darkness, only occasionally diluted by moving flashes of railway signal lamps behind a small window – read Helena Blavatsky's *The Secret Doctrine*.

It took the funeral train less than an hour to complete its sad and unhurried twenty-three-mile journey to Brookwood Cemetery. Yadwiga, Melissa and Bulgakov were the only passengers to disembark at first stop, the Brookwood North Station, around which were burial grounds for non-Anglican "dissenters": Catholics, Jews, Pharisees and even Zoroastrians were located here. The ethnically cleansed train, now with a purely Anglican load of both dead and living passengers, then proceeded to Brookwood South Station, leaving our heroes on a dark empty platform, separated from the cemetery fence by a short flight of stairs.

"I am pleased that journey is over," said Melissa. "I will probably never die, but being surrounded by all those tearful black-clad mourners felt spooky."

"And I enjoyed the ride very much!" exclaimed Bulgakov. "I have always wanted to find out more about Helena Blavatsky's take on the three main principles of the occult!"

"We must now find the cemetery's office," cut in Yadwiga, with a touch of irony in her voice. "And we don't have all night!"

"Yes, but before we do so, we must return to our Bookland reality, because we don't want to be looking at a hundred-year-old edition of *The Surrey Book of the Dead*," Bulgakov remarked.

"Tell us how we do it," Yadwiga demanded assertively.

"I am glad you didn't formulate it as a question," said the Cat. "There is no better way than reading from *Granny Yaga* – the book which we all come from. Only in this case, I won't be able to offer you a peep into the future and tell you what's going to happen next. The reason is simple: we are now part of the plot in progress. The

Writer is trying to describe our next steps, words and actions literally as we speak, and at this point he would bend over backwards to not give away too much to the readers, who are bound to lose interest in the story if they learn how it ends before it actually ends. Particularly so if the end of the book is just one chapter away. As fairly independent literary characters we can get away with nearly anything. One thing we can never do, though, is go against the Writer's intentions, and by those I mean both his plot and his imagination, simply because it is inside them – and nowhere else – that we all actually exist!"

"If so, just read us any extract you can get hold of – and fast," said Yadwiga.

"As I have just said, I can't offer you the future, but I'll try to give you the present instead," Bulgakov muttered mysteriously and jumped up in the air. When he landed on his hind legs, in his front paws was a freshly printed copy of *Granny Yaga*. He opened it, and even in the faint light of the stars above the platform, Melissa and Yadwiga could see that the page he was staring at was totally empty. Bulgakov opened his mouth slightly – and small printed letters started running onto the white surface of the page from somewhere inside the book's spine, like a line of ants from a small tree trunk hollow. The first line was followed by the next one, and then the next, as the Cat kept reading…

"They got off the platform and found themselves on the edge of a huge cemetery – Europe's largest burial ground, in fact. At the gate, there was a billboard with a cemetery map, lit up by a lantern. They were relieved that inside it was a modern luminescent light bulb, no longer a gas wick from the early 1900s. Bulgakov's trick had worked again, and they were back in modern Bookland.

According to the map, the office was about a ten-minute walk away. To get there, they had to take Railway Avenue (yes, the cemetery had its own avenues, streets, squares and roads – a real city of the dead!) then cut across some empty meadows where lots of burial space was still available and unclaimed.

They walked in silence among tombstones – past the laurels, ferns and old conifers lining Railway Avenue. In her right hand, Yadwiga was holding a small bottle with the Water of Life from the cauldron of their birth. Before flying to Crouch End, she had made a brief foray to Yesterdayland via the perfectly functioning Ely Place portal and fetched a small bottle of the Water of Life to revive her sister in case she was indeed dead. There was no guarantee, however, that the water was going to work: after more than a thousand years, it could have gone past its use-by date and lost all its magic qualities.

Tall cemetery trees were throwing black moving shadows on our heroes' faces as they walked along Railway Avenue, winding among the graves. Gentle rustling could be heard in the bushes, and an invisible owl was hooting monotonously in the distance.

"I… I am scared of ghosts…" Bulgakov mumbled.

"Look who is talking!" said Yadwiga. "A cat who has just spent an hour reading obliviously inside a dark funeral carriage among coffins! Even *Kikimora*, demon of the night, would feel uneasy in that kind of environment!"

"I am not afraid of the dead, only of ghosts, who are not quite dead," objected Bulgakov.

"Shame on you! As an intelligent and well-read animal, you should know that ghosts do not exist," insisted Yadwiga.

"Next you'll say that *ved'mas* and learned Cats do not exist either," Bulgakov kept grumbling.

The cemetery office occupied a detached Arts and Crafts bungalow with a satellite dish on the tiled roof. Not a flicker of light could be seen in any of its windows. On the locked front door, they spotted a hand-written sign, which Bulgakov, using his night-vision skills, was able to read without effort:

"The Surrey Book of the Dead" is out of print. We don't have a copy and cannot answer any enquiries as to its contents.

"Well, according to PC Farnham, the only other option is finding the Orthodox monks of St Edward's Monastery," Melissa said with a sigh.

The monastery was next to the South Station of the Necropolis Railway at the opposite end of the cemetery. To get there, they had to take St Jude's Avenue and walk past the burial plots of many different nations and confessions: Catholic, Swedish, Turkish, Arabic and even Zoroastrian. An "actors' graveyard" was on their way too.

"No matter how nice and helpful those Orthodox monks can be, I don't think they will be too happy to be woken up in the middle of the night by two witches and a black cat… St Jude's Avenue… No wonder St Jude was the patron saint of hopeless causes…" mumbled Bulgakov as they were walking past Polish, Latvian and other East European graves.

"Stop moaning, Bulgakov, and keep moving!" snapped Yadwiga.

But they didn't have to go much further.

"Look at this!" Melissa, who was ahead, exclaimed suddenly. "I think I can see her name here, or maybe I am hallucinating…"

She was squinting at a white marble tombstone of a modest grave, with no wreaths or flowers on it, struggling to read the epitaph.

"I left my reading glasses in the shop, and it is too dark for me see it clearly," she lamented.

"It says 'Lucinda Yaghina,' but there are no dates," Bulgakov announced from behind her back. "There's something else underneath it too."

He came closer, bent down and read out loud:

Do not stand at my grave and cry.

I am not here. I did not die.

"I don't understand," said Melissa. "I don't understand what it all means!"

Yadwiga kept looking at the grave in silence for a minute or two. Then she said: "It means that Lucinda has left us a message. She is telling us she was in mortal danger, and this grave is here to mislead her enemy or enemies into believing that she had indeed died, whereas in fact she has managed to survive, thank Perun!"

"Thank Perun!" echoed Melissa.

"I can also assure you," continued Yadwiga, "that this epitaph is intended for our eyes only and will vanish from the tombstone the moment we walk away."

"Yes, I can see it now. It is so like Lucinda – caring, inventive and ingenious!" exclaimed Melissa.

"Not so sure about the 'caring' bit, sister. Had she really cared about us, she wouldn't have been out of touch for hundreds of years!"

"But let's face it; we were the same, Yadwiga! You didn't even bother to pop into the shop to say hi when you came to England in 1843. I don't blame you: you were too much in love with your writer from Knebworth to find time to see your sister! So let's not judge Lucinda too harshly. At least now she is telling us not to worry about her anymore."

"You are right, Melissa," agreed Yadwiga. "We must hurry back to your shop, find the egg and put an end to Koshchei's terror – once and for all. Then, I am sure, we'll finally be reunited with Lucinda too."

They were pacing back to Brookwood North Station along Railway Avenue and were unable to see how the epitaph on the tombstone was getting bleaker and bleaker, its letters fading away by the minute until, at last, they disappeared completely – like lumps of sugar in a bowl of hot porridge. By the time the first light of dawn descended on Brookwood Cemetery, the polished marble surface underneath the name looked pristine and untouched. Then Lucinda's name disappeared too and was replaced by: "Lydia Rosina, wife of Samuel Grimes, 1803–1896."

They took the 05:23 modern South West Trains service back to London and were ten minutes into their return journey when Bulgakov stopped reading from *Granny Yaga*. It was the first train of the day to arrive at Waterloo, at 06.12 am. As Bulgakov began to nod off, lulled by the carriage's soporific rocking, the book slid out of his paws. It never reached the floor of their second-class carriage, but simply vanished halfway through the fall. Neither the Cat nor the sisters noticed its disappearance, simply because all three of them were fast asleep. Or, possibly, were simply resting with their eyes closed…"

It looked as if — tired by the adventures of the day — everyone else was asleep, not just in the "normal" modern world, but in Bookland and Yesterdayland too. The only person still awake was the Writer. Bent over his desk inside the garden office in his leafy Hertfordshire town, he was forcefully — almost angrily — pounding the keyboard of his laptop.

Chapter Seventeen

In which Yadwiga is reunited with her old flying kit, and Danya celebrates his eleventh birthday

BEFORE flying to Bloomsbury, Yadwiga and Melissa briefly returned to Crouch End to pick up their Dysons. Bulgakov travelled with them to Crouch End, but refused to accompany the sisters on their flight to Central London. Suffering from vertigo, he didn't like the idea of being a passenger on top of a flying vacuum cleaner, no matter how cutting edge it was. He said he was tired and would rather get back to Yesterdayland to catch a nap in the Hut on chicken's feet.

It was mid-morning when the sisters reached Bloomsbury. Needless to say they did not find the egg with Koshchei's life in it. The wall in the Runes bookshop basement did slide apart at the first mention of "Juba" ("Thanks, Edward, darling!", thought Yadwiga), but the only thing they discovered in the cache inside the magic corridor behind it was a hastily scribbled note addressed to Yadwiga:

By the time you read this, the egg is going to be very far away. Don't even try to find it ever again. Enjoy the remaining few years of your life! Immortally yours, KTD (Koshchei the Deathless).

Koshchei's personal signature – a miniature live spider stirring its tiny legs tirelessly – was underneath the message.

Yadwiga squashed the spider with her thumb and looked up at Melissa.

"Cheeky old scoundrel! But you know what: Lucinda is alive, and this makes me so happy that I couldn't care less about the egg. At least at the moment I couldn't! And I am not afraid of dying either, as long as I know that both you and Lucinda, my two beloved sisters, are safe."

"Come off it, Yadwiga!" Melissa said with mock irritation. "We will find the egg one day. It was what Lucinda told me when I saw her last!"

"Yes, I remember, but by the time it happens, I may be dead."

"You won't be, sister! You have to carry on for our sake and for the sake of the Sablins. You are so lucky to have a family when both Lucinda and I are lonely. Just be patient and try to stay away from questions and questioning for a bit longer – that is all it takes!"

There was nothing else for them to do in the basement. The sisters went up the stairs and the solid concrete wall closed silently behind them.

Back in the shop, Yadwiga turned her mobile on and saw a missed call icon on its monitor. Someone called while they were in the basement where there was no reception and her phone was therefore both switched and witched off.

Yadwiga recognised Irina's number and pressed the "call back" button.

It was Danya who answered the phone.

"Granny, you've been away for too long and I miss you," he said.

Yadwiga realised it was Danya's tactful way of avoiding the direct "Where are you and when are you coming back?" questions and thought what a wonderfully caring boy he was. "I am still with my sister Melissa," she said. "And you must be at school."

"It's my birthday today, and Mum and Dad allowed me to stay at home!" he announced cheerfully.

"Because of the cursed egg hunt I have forgotten Danya's eleventh birthday! Shame on me!" thought Yadwiga. "And I haven't even got a present for him yet!"

"I called you from Mum's phone," continued Danya, and Yadwiga suddenly knew what she would get him for his birthday. "I just wanted to say that Pani Czerniowiecka is back, and Mum and Dad decided that we should all leave her house tonight. Also, Mr Humphrey Smith from the British Museum, whom I met during the school trip, phoned this morning to ask you to see him at his office immediately. Please, Granny, get home soon!"

"I will be back by lunchtime," she promised.

* * *

The British Museum was across the road from the shop. Making her way through the ever-so-crowded courtyard, Yadwiga was reminded of her evening flight above it five months earlier and realised she was missing her old mortar and pestle flying kit which had served her faithfully for over a thousand years.

At the entrance, a burly guard with the nametag "Atlas Halliday" on his chest directed her to staff reception, and soon Humphrey Smith, in his regulation tweed-and-bowtie outfit, came out to greet her.

"Lovely to meet you, Mrs Sablina," he said shaking Yadwiga's hand. "Thanks for coming and please follow me to my office."

"It's Miss, not Mrs, and Yaghina, not Sablina," Yadwiga corrected him.

"Terribly sorry, Ms Yaghina," apologised Humphrey, and to get away from this sensitive subject, added: "I had the pleasure to meet your lovely grandson the other day. A very intelligent boy!"

Humphrey Smith's small curatorial office on the third floor of the staff wing was brimming with old books and manuscripts. A disproportionally large oak wardrobe, taking up almost half of the room, stood in the corner. Having cleared some space on his desk top by shoving a tall pile of papers off it and onto the floor, he offered Yadwiga a drink of pale tepid tea in a battered mug with dark brown stains under the rim. He then walked back to the door, which was half ajar, and closed it thoroughly.

"What a truly amazing morning I am having," he said, having sat in a swivel chair opposite Yadwiga. "Literally an hour ago, a man with an extremely well-made copy of an Imperial Fabergé egg came to see me. I don't have to tell you how rare and valuable these eggs are. He said he had discovered the egg by accident among other possessions of his recently deceased grandfather, of whom he was allegedly the only heir, and offered it to the museum for one million pounds – a very reasonable sum, considering that the Imperial Eggs are very rare and literally priceless. I consulted all relevant catalogues, but was unable to find that particular egg in any, which made me think that it was a beautifully executed copy rather than an original. So I directed the man to Edinburgh, where a "Fabulous Fabergé" exhibition is now underway at the Queen's Gallery of the Holyroodhouse Palace. The curator is, incidentally, an old friend of mine..."

"My second egg drama of the morning! How interesting!" thought Yadwiga. "It could be one and the same egg, of course. If so, Koshchei may not be in possession of his life and death receptacle any longer, and what a crafty – in more than one sense! – idea to camouflage the egg with his life as a Fabergé egg!"

"There must be a reason for you to be telling me this story first thing on my arrival," she said aloud.

"Absolutely!" Humphrey Smith confirmed with a smile. He was very impressed by the old lady's directness, shrewdness and assertiveness, all of which made him even more certain that she was indeed who he thought she was. "Absolutely! And you will find out all about it in just a minute."

He stood up and took a couple of steps towards the wardrobe in the corner.

"I have reason to believe we have something that belongs to you inside this wardrobe," he continued.

From the pocket of his tweed jacket, he took out a small key, opened the wardrobe's squeaky door and invited Yadwiga to come over.

She could not believe her eyes: inside, her faithful mortar and pestle were floating slowly up and down, as if dancing with joy at the sight of their mistress.

Yadwiga was close to tears. She shut her eyes and hummed softly in Slavonian:

Stupushka, matushka,
Shagai shir'ye -
versti po chetir'ye...
My little mother mortar,
start pacing widely –
four miles in each step...

It was her old way of enticing her kit to start moving. And, as if they recognised the words (which they did), the pestle jumped inside the mortar – and together they tried to fly out of the wardrobe through the open door which Humphrey Smith had to shut and lock hastily.

"Dear Miss Yaghina, I know who you are!" he announced when they were back at his desk. "Since childhood, I have been your devoted fan and admirer, although I have to admit, at times I was a bit scared of you too. I can't express in words how delighted I am to meet the real Baba Yaga! And I can see very clearly that you are not scary at all!"

"That's very nice of you, Mr Smith," said Yadwiga. "But now you know who I am, I hope I can have my flying kit back."

"Of course you can, of course, but... it is not as simple as it seems. Since initially we thought that it belonged to no-one, it is now on the museum's inventory as part of the ongoing East European folklore exhibition. And it has been the absolute highlight, I have to add. I've managed to smuggle it out to my office for an hour or so, but even that wasn't easy. It would be much more difficult to explain to my superiors that I have returned the precious exhibit to its rightful owner – Baba Yaga. They would never believe it and would be likely to think I've lost my marbles and probably sack me!"

Yadwiga was listening without interrupting.

"Also, to be absolutely honest, I find it hard to imagine what practical use you can make in modern times out of that spectacular, yet totally outdated, flying apparatus," Humphrey Smith continued.

"The traffic in the skies above London is crazy, and no matter how colourful and memorable your old kit can be, it is slow, wobbly and bound to attract lots of unwanted attention."

He stood up from his desk again and was pacing up and down his cubicle of an office, like a prisoner confined to a tiny cell.

"To cut a long story short, I want to make you an offer which I hope you won't refuse. Here at the museum, we have some funds to acquire objects of high artistic and historical importance for our collections. Of course, we have to be very careful with the British taxpayers' money, but it so happens that some of it can be spared at the moment, and I would have been very tempted to authorise paying the requested sum to my earlier visitor, had I been able to properly authenticate the object he had shown me. That was why I told you about this morning's encounter. I would be more than happy now to offer the same sum of one million pounds to you if I can persuade you to bequeath your flying kit to our museum, so that it could continue to be admired by the public worldwide – please forgive my unintended pomposity. I must confess that I have a personal interest here too: I have just started writing a dissertation under the title *Metaphors, Signs and Symbols of Defiance in Pagan Folklore* and further studies of your unique apparatus would be of enormous help here. I am also hoping you'd agree to act as the museum's freelance consultant on matters of paganism and East European culture. We'd be able to offer you a small retainer for that, although if you were to accept my previous offer, you'd probably be happy to forsake it!"

He fell silent and looked at Yadwiga, who was staring at the floor and not saying anything.

"So what do you think, Ms Yaghina?"

Yadwiga shuddered.

"If you really knew about me, you should be aware that I do not take questions very well!" she said angrily.

"Please forgive me, Ms Yaghina," Humphrey pleaded. "Your dislike of direct questions is very familiar to me; I simply got carried away by all the possibilities of our hypothetical collaboration."

"Never mind: one wrinkle more, one wrinkle less," Yadwiga said in a conciliatory voice. "I've been thinking about your offer, and to be honest, had you made it even yesterday I would have rejected it straight away. But recent developments in my adopted family and some other personal circumstances that came up literally as we spoke indicate I may be in for a lot of travels and travel expenses in the very near future. Besides, when I thought that my mortar and pestle had been lost for good, on my sister's advice I acquired a somewhat more modern flying device, and, to be honest, have been enjoying it immensely."

"I promise we are going to look after your old kit very well here," said Humphrey. "And you can come to test fly it, or just to say hi, any time – I will make special provisions for that, I promise!"

It was now Yadwiga's turn to stand up and come up to the wardrobe:

"*Prosti menia, stupushka*," she uttered, with her lips pressed closely to the door. "Forgive me, my little mortar. I am not abandoning you forever and will be coming to see you often!"

She then turned to Humphrey Smith, watching her in stunned anticipation.

"We've got a deal here," she said. "Or rather two deals at once. And you can keep your retainer!"

Soon she was back in the Runes, or rather in the shop's minuscule backyard where – on a small paved patio – her blue Dyson was parked next to Melissa's red one. Yadwiga sat astride it, typed her destination on the liquid-crystal GPS screen and, having firmly depressed the "start" button, took off towards North London.

* * *

Forty miles away, in Hertfordshire, the Writer stretched, yawned and stood up from his desk. He noted with a smile that in the last paragraphs of the book he made Humphrey Smith stand up from HIS desk several times in quick succession. A bit of wishful thinking on his part, for he himself was so eager to stretch his legs after a whole night of writing. Now it was all over. At least, for the time being... Well, almost... He needed some rest before the evening when he was planning to attend a birthday party.

* * *

Danya's eleventh birthday party was held in the vast lounge room of Pani Czerniowiecka's house – the very house that had harboured the Sablins for nearly five months and which they were about to leave.

The whole family, including Yadwiga, plus Pani Czerniowiecka, the landlady, were seated at a solid oak extension table, sagging under plates with traditional East European party snacks: aubergine caviar, *pierogi*, beetroot-coated herring – the so-called "herring in a fur coat" – potato pancakes, salad Olivier... In the middle of the table was the main dish of the evening – a huge oval plate with a crispy shepherd's pie, freshly baked by Irina as a tribute to the culinary traditions of their adopted country.

The bay windows in the lounge room were open and cheerful chirping of birds could be heard from the garden. One distinctive multi-pitched voice stood out in that evening chorus: it was a nightingale warming up for a mellifluous all-night solo.

The conversation at the table was stilted. The Sablins were saddened by their impending departure from the house and from the city they had come to love. With the exception of the birthday boy himself, who was engrossed in Yadwiga's present – a brand new mobile phone with a secret "witch on" function – they were all somewhat embarrassed by the silent presence of Pani Czerniowiecka, semi-transparent and strapped to her chair, with her permanently half-open (or rather half-shut) eyes staring down at the floor.

Yadwiga was hoping that the arrival of Melissa, who had also been invited, would lighten up the atmosphere. Bulgakov had insisted on coming over too. He pleaded so much that Yadwiga finally gave in, but only on very strict conditions: he would pose as Melissa's pet cat, would be kept on a lead and wouldn't utter a single word or try to read anything, not even a newspaper, while at the party. But Melissa and her "pet" were running late…

Yadwiga decided to take the initiative.

"I am pleased we all have agreed to spend some time in Edinburgh," she said. "It is a beautiful city, and the kids are going to like it. As for me, I have a small personal matter to attend to there."

"Please tell us again what WE are going to do in Edinburgh," asked Sergei.

"Same as here, if that's what you fancy," shrugged Yadwiga. "Good handymen are in demand everywhere. But, if you feel like not working and taking it easy for a while, you are welcome, too. I told you already that I had unexpectedly inherited a lump sum from a distant relative who had just passed away, and would gladly share it with you, so that we could all do a bit of travelling and sightseeing."

"And we can have a break from school too! This sounds great!" exclaimed Danya without looking up from the screen of his new phone.

"No way!" Irina retorted. "You and Olga will carry on with your studies no matter what!"

"Sure enough," muttered Olga, who until now, had been sulking silently over her untouched meal. "First, they take us away from our friends and then they start dictating to us what to do. As if neither Hobbit nor myself have any say in this matter. As if we don't actually exist…"

"This is how I feel too!" Pani Czerniowiecka echoed suddenly from her seat. "No-one asked *my* opinion about it all!"

She was speaking in a very weak monotonous voice without lifting up or fully opening her eyes, and her jelly-like, see-through body stirred with every word.

"As a matter of fact, I am now alive too and am going to stay alive for a whole year, even if at times I do not seem as if I am," she carried on. "I am an eternal pariah – too dead for the living, too alive for the dead – and not accepted by either as a result. I know exactly why you are leaving: you simply cannot stand having me around. And I don't blame you – I can be scary, I can be difficult, but more than anything I am *different*, and anyone different from the majority is destined to be a loner!"

The Sablins and Yadwiga did not know what to say, so they said nothing while Pani Czerniowiecka continued her monologue:

"But I want you to know that we *mamunas* – dead or alive – have souls too. We like laughter, we like fun, we like company. And although we come from the swamps of Bialowiecki Forest, these are the world's most beautiful marshes. As the great Polish poet Adam Mickiewicz wrote:

Beyond these pools, it is vain to try to penetrate even with the eye, to say nothing of one's steps, for there all is covered with a misty cloud that rises incessantly from quivering morasses. But finally behind the mist... extends a very fair and fertile region, the main capital of the kingdom of beasts and plants...

To everyone's unspoken relief, an ear-piercing doorbell ring interrupted Pani Czerniowiecka's truly spirited (for what else could it be when delivered by an actual spirit?) declamation.

Sergei rushed out to answer the door, and a moment later Melissa entered the lounge room. On a lead behind her was a very large black cat with intelligent green eyes.

"Please meet my twin sister Melissa and her pet cat Bulgakov!" said Yadwiga. At this point, Irina, who sat closest to the newcomers, thought she could hear the cat cough out very quietly, as if clearing his throat, but she couldn't be sure.

"Yadwiga must be getting senile," she was thinking. "Twin sister... Melissa looks at least forty years younger than her!"

As if Yadwiga could read Irina's thoughts (she could!), she suddenly realised her mistake and added: "Sorry, I meant my younger sister of course."

"How lovely to meet you all," smiled Melissa. "Yadwiga told me so much about you! And look what I've got for the birthday boy!"

From her handbag she took out a parcel and handed it over to Danya. He hastily tore off the wrapping paper.

"Oooh, it's pyjamas," he droned with badly concealed disappointment. "Thank you so much, Auntie Melissa!"

"It is a very special pyjamas set," said Melissa. "But to understand how special, you must put it on first."

Reluctantly – just trying to be polite – Danya trundled off to his room to change.

Melissa installed herself at the table, with Bulgakov stretched (rather reluctantly, or so it seemed) on the floor under her chair.

"Shall I pour some milk for your cat?" asked Olga.

"Don't worry, dear. I fed him shortly before we flew here…"

"What do you mean by 'we flew'? I didn't realise we had a small airport in the backyard…"

"Did I say 'flew'? How silly of me… We took the Tube of course, but were in such a hurry to get here that it appeared as if we were indeed flying – ha-ha-ha!"

Melissa was saved from further embarrassment by Danya who actually FLEW into the lounge room – giggling and waving his hands in the air as if they were wings.

"Mummy, Daddy, look at me: I am flying! I am flying!"

He bounced off the ceiling and was now swinging from Pani Czerniowiecka's imperial brass chandelier.

"Danya, be careful! Don't fall!" screamed Irina.

"Don't worry, he won't," said Yadwiga. "These are special flying pyjamas, which Melissa bought for Danya on my advice. They are absolutely safe and may actually help him avoid all sorts of small domestic accidents in the future…"

She looked up at Danya, still astride the chandelier, and winked at him quickly and almost imperceptibly. He understood immediately that Granny was trying to remind him of the memorable plastic fruit episode several years earlier when she caught him as he fell off the pyramid of chairs and saved his life.

"But what if he flies out of the house and gets carried away by the wind?" Irina asked worriedly.

"That is impossible," Melissa intervened. "The flying pyjamas are programmed to work indoors only. An inbuilt safety switch automatically disables the flying function when outside."

The doorbell was ringing again.

"Who can that be? We weren't expecting anyone else," Irina said to no-one in particular as Sergei went to answer the door.

"It is a postman!" he shouted from the corridor. "He's got a special delivery birthday card for Danya!"

"Do ask him to come in," said Irina.

A short broad-shouldered man, wearing a red Royal Mail jacket, entered the room. He was holding a sealed envelope in his hand.

When Bulgakov saw the postman, he was ready to jump up in the air and meow loudly with surprise. And he would have definitely done so, had he not been positioned under Melissa's chair and held down tightly by the lead. The Cat was the only one in the room who knew what the Writer looked like, for he had seen a photo of him on the back flap of one of his previous books – *Life as a Literary Device* – from the door of his garden office. There could be no mistake!

"Can I see Master Daniil Sablin?" asked the Writer, dressed as a postman, and added: "I need his signature to confirm delivery."

"I'll be down in a tic," Danya's voice sounded from above.

The postman-cum-Writer looked up and saw a boy hanging on to the chandelier.

"Daniil, fly immediately to your room and change into normal clothes!" commanded Sergei. Danya nodded, pushed himself away from the ceiling with his feet, made a somersault in the air, and – laughing and waving his hands frantically – flew out into the corridor.

He soon walked back in and, having scribbled two large and round letters, "D" and "S," in the postman's dog-eared register, opened the envelope.

"It is from Auntie Lucinda, another sister of Granny Yadwiga!" he announced before reading the card aloud:

Happy Birthday to Danya! Long live life!
Lucinda

"Why don't you sit down and have a drink and something to eat?" Irina suggested to the postman. "I don't know what we are going to do with all this food: we are all leaving for the airport in half an hour, and Pani Czerniowiecka here is not much of an eater…"

"Not for the first couple of months after the grave," Pani Czerniowiecka confirmed from her seat in a feeble monotonous voice.

"Very kind of you, ma'am!" said the postman. "I think I will accept your invitation. It's the end of my shift anyway…"

He sat down on a vacant chair next to the *mamuna* and put some aubergine caviar on his plate.

"In Slavonia, we used to call it 'poor man's caviar'," Sergei explained with a friendly grin.

"It is absolutely delicious, and the taste is rich, not poor!" said the Writer-cum-postman with his mouth full.

Shortly before the departure, Irina brought in Danya's favourite layered custard cake, "Napoleon", which she and Olga had baked together. Eleven burning candles were proudly sticking out of it, and Danya blew them all out with one mighty puff – to everyone's applause. At that point, it appeared to Olga that Auntie Melissa's cat was again behaving strangely under the chair – rubbing his front paws together when everyone was clapping, as if applauding too. Just like her mother earlier, she was not entirely sure: he could simply be scratching, as cats do…

But when everyone, including the postman and Pani Czernionwiecka, burst into singing "Happy Birthday!" Olga's doubts grew. She kept watching the cat from the corner of her eye and could vouch that he was opening his little mouth in unison with the tune. At some point, she thought she could even hear him droning in a very weak high-pitched falsetto: "Happy Birthday, dear Danya! Happy Birthday to you-oo!"

Luckily for Bulgakov, neither Olga not anyone else at the party had time to ponder over the cat's behaviour. The Sablins had a plane to catch, and Melissa and Pani Czerniowiecka were both eager to see them off at the airport. Yadwiga toyed again with the idea of commandeering the AER from the neighbouring house under the guise of a flying cab, as she did several months earlier to take Sergei and Irina home from the police station, but they told her at number 127 that the Astral Energy Receiver had been heavily booked for the evening. A normal London black cab had to be called in its stead, and they all managed to squeeze in with their luggage, except for Bulgakov.

"Can I leave my cat at your house and pick him up on the way back from the airport?" Melissa asked Pani Czerniowiecka.

"No problem," replied the *mamuna*. "I like the fact that a living being will be in my house while I am away. I could then imagine he had been waiting for me. No-one ever waits for me, except perhaps for the Highgate Vampire at the cemetery, but he is extremely selfish and has only one bloody thing on his mind. That was why I was so happy to have the Slavonian family as my tenants."

"We may still come back," said Irina. She was now feeling a lot of sympathy for the lonely creature, who no longer looked scary to her. But it was too late to change their plans.

As the cab driver switched on the ignition, the dragon on the roof of house number 125 (that was Snake Horinich of course) stirred and lifted its right front paw slightly above the parapet, as if to wave goodbye. And when the cab started moving, a black-clad knight on a coal-black horse materialised from nowhere and rode ten yards behind the car – like a silent escort – all the way to Heathrow as night was slowly setting in.

Epilogue

INSIDE the house, which suddenly felt very empty, Bulgakov climbed out from under the chair.

"Can you please take this blasted lead off me?" he asked the Writer.

"That's better!" said the Cat with relief when the lead was off. "I had cramps all over my body while crouched under that chair!"

He stretched, jumped onto the table, and, having picked up a knife, cut himself a large piece of Napoleon cake. He then looked at the Writer.

"Why did you gate-crash the party?"

"Just wanted to meet everyone properly, I suppose," the Writer shrugged. "Thought it would be nice to be able to say again, 'I was there too, but the beer and the mead only wetted my non-existing whiskers – and not a drop ended up in my mouth', as I did in the Prologue. You know what we writers are like... We crave symmetry... And talking about gate-crashing, didn't you turn up uninvited too?"

"Guilty as charged," sighed Bulgakov, his little mouth full of custard. "So what's next?"

"No idea. I will only know the answer when I get back home and resume writing."

When the door closed behind the "postman", Bulgakov slowly finished his cake. He then installed himself on the soft lounge room sofa. From under one of its cushions, he ferreted out a book, with "Granny Yaga in Edinburgh" on its cover, and opened it.

The page he was staring at was blank.

Hertfordshire, 2011 – 2012

Turn to the back for an extract from the next Granny Yaga book…

From the Author

A LL grown-ups were once children… but only few of them remember it," Antoine de Saint-Exupéry, a great French writer, pilot and fantasist, wrote in *The Little Prince*.

With this beautiful thought in mind, I ventured to subtitle *Granny Yaga* "A Fantasy Novel for Children and Adults" – a very cheeky thing to do from many a publisher's point of view.

I also did it with the knowledge that *Granny Yaga* had been equally enjoyed by both children and adults, at least by all those children and adults to whom I showed the manuscript prior to publication.

Indeed, statistics assert that more and more adults now resort to reading children's books, whereas children – starting from early teens – are often more keen on the so-called "grown-up" literature and "chapter books" than on their old diet of comics and fairy tales. This process of disappearing borders between children's and adult's literature has become known as "The Harry Potter Phenomenon", according to BBC Radio 4.

"Children are not frightened of words they don't know," Francesca Simon, the award-winning author of *Horrid Henry*, wrote in *The Guardian* on 17 September 2013 (in the article "Ten tips to make bedtime reading fun") and explained: "*Swallows and Amazons* [a classic children's novel by Arthur Ransome – VV] is filled with arcane language – I had no idea what many of the sailing terms meant. After reading half a page of gibberish, I told my son I hadn't understood many of the words. 'Neither did I, but I liked them,' he said."

To me "The Harry Potter Phenomenon" makes every sense. While writing *Granny Yaga*, I tried not to sound patronising to either children or adults and to speak to both in the language I normally speak myself – at work and at home. If when reading my book, a child comes across a word he or she does not understand, they could always ask their parents or grandparents to provide an explanation – at least this is what most of us used to do when we were children. It is what I call learning while bonding, or rather bonding while learning, and I simply cannot think of a better way to learn or to bond.

And while most publishers are still stubbornly segregating (or "separating") children from adults and younger children from older children, this book has a double purpose: to remind adults that they were children, and to forewarn children of their quickly approaching adulthood.

Vitali Vitaliev

About the Author

VITALI Vitaliev was born in 1954 in Kharkiv, Ukraine. He first made a name for himeself in the then Soviet Union, writing satirical journalism in *Krokadil* and other publications, exposing the activies of organised crime and the all-permeating corruption in the collapsing country. His fearless stance ultimately led to his defection in 1990, following months of persecution by the KGB.

He has appeared regularly on TV and radio in the UK (*Have I Got News For You, Saturday Night Clive, Today, Start the Week*), was a writer/researcher for *QI* and has contributed to newspapers and magazines all over the world.

He is the author of eleven books, written in English and translated into a number of foreign languages, including German, Japanese, Russian and Italian.

Vitali now lives in Herfordshire, where he is working on the next book about Granny Yaga. Turn the page to read an extract.

"Vitaliev has a sharp and sardonic eye; and his observations are informed by his humanity and compassion." *Daily Telegraph*

"Vitali Vitaliev is a star in the making."
Time magazine

"Vitaliev has an irrepressible sense of humour"
The *Guardian*

This is an edited extract from the second part of the "Granny Yaga" trilogy planned by the author...

GRANNY YAGA IN AULD REEKIE
Chapter One

In which Yadwiga and Bulgakov make an appearance at the Edinburgh International Festival of Magic, the Sablins familiarise themselves with their Tardis-style hotel and Koshchei chills out in Chillingham Castle across the border

H ere we start!" announced the magician. From the pocket of his black frock he produced a stack of playing cards and threw it up in the air. Instead of tumbling down messily on the floor, the cards mysteriously stuck together, then flew apart in wedge-like formations, like flocks of some mysterious - flat and rectangular - migratory birds. Having floated above the stage for a minute or so, the cards folded back into a stack and landed smoothly onto the magician's outstretched palm. The audience burst into applause...

It was the first night of the Edinburgh International Magic Festival, and the Royal Lyceum Theatre, where the opening gala show was held, was full to the bursting point. The Magic Festival was a recent addition to the city's numerous events in the fields of science, books, performing arts, circus and whatnot that lasted almost all year round. Not to mention the world's largest Fringe Festival every August when the whole of Old Edinburgh would turn into one giant theatre, with hundreds of stages on which performances were happening round the clock – a Festival City indeed.

That year the Magic Festival had attracted a number of world-famous magicians.

Among them were:

- the inimitable American Chuck Dworkin, nicknamed Torpedo, who repeatedly brought the whole of Manhattan to a stand-still by effortlessly levitating above the Fifth Avenue;
- the extremely popular – almost of a rock-star fame – Daniel Maine, who once spend two months in a tightly sealed glass cabin, suspended high above the River Seine in Paris, without food or water, surviving only by drinking his own urine and ignoring the skeptics who tried to question the origins of that very urine;
- the clairvoyant Micky Ray, who was able to name correctly any card picked out by his interlocutor over the phone – from thousands of miles away;
- And last but not least, Sven Takanava – a follower of Harry Houdini who made headlines by escaping from a specially constructed "Cherry Wood Box of Death", submerged 300 feet under water, with his hands handcuffed and his feet shackled.

Alongside these world-famous illusionists, the Magic Festival had brought together dozens of aspiring and hopeful practitioners of magic – men and women – with their top hats, under which doves, rabbits and miles of brightly coloured ribbon were dwelling; with their differently shaped *gibeciere* (magicians' chests), "jackets of doom", "curtains of death", and coffin-shaped wooden crates, in which young women in spangled dresses would be sawed in two, without any visible damage to their make-up and their blissful smiles... The competition for the highly desired Great Lafayette Award, which only one winner was going to receive, was expected to be tough, and the audience was watching breathlessly as the participants were taking turns to demonstrate their truly amazing skills.

As at most similar events, the first two rows in the otherwise packed theatre hall were empty. The reason was that, according to a popular belief, those seated in the front rows were more likely to be picked up by the performers, called up on stage and subsequently embarrassed, possibly even humiliated, by having some intimate details of their lives revealed and their possessions taken away by the magicians.

"If you think that you are safe in the back rows, you are wrong!" It was Boris Monsoon, the next performer, acclaimed for his legendary mastery of *legerdemain* (dexterity of hands). He never wore a jacket on stage and always performed in short sleeves, with his hands and wrists exposed to the public to alleviate any suspicions of foul play. But he always wore a top hat.

"Don't worry, I am not going to invite you on stage only to make your watch disappear. Nor am I planning to cut through your torso with a saw," Boris was saying to the muffled accompaniment of Berlioz' *Symphonie Fantastique*. "Those are old cheap tricks, not worthy of the magician of my calibre, or in other words, a very accomplished cheat (at this point, several timid cackles could be heard from the audience). "My magic is going to reach everyone, particularly those in the back rows. But only a handful of you, the unlucky ones, will be directly affected – I promise!"

He took off his hat and waved it in the air. A couple of wood pigeons flew out of it and started dashing to and fro under the ceiling.

"Cover up your heads, ladies and gentlemen!" Boris cried out with a sinister grin on his face. For a couple of people in the audience, however, the call came a bit too late – a fraction of a second later than a sprinkle of the frightened birds' blue-ish droppings hit the crowns of their heads. The unaffected part of the audience was dying with laughter...

Boris opened his mouth to utter another well-rehearsed banality of the type: "Well, I am not sure about the Lafayette, but some unasked-for awards have just been distributed, it appears..." when a hoarse, yet very loud, voice which, by the sound of it, belonged to an old woman, roared from the audience: "And he calls it magic! What a disgrace!!"

All heads turned towards the voice. A diminutive old lady in a bright-red kerchief stood up from her seat in the stalls and was slowly making her way towards the stage. She was followed by a very large black cat walking on his hind legs and mumbling softly to no-one in particular: "My apologies, sir... sorry to disturb you, madam... thanks for letting us pass..."

With his mouth wide open, Boris watched the old lady and the cat climb up the stage. "Would you be so kind as to..." he began but was unable to finish. In full view of the mesmerised audience, he suddenly began to shrink rapidly, getting smaller and smaller by the moment until he became no more than a couple of inches tall. Incredibly, his shiny shoes, his shirt, trousers and even his magician's top hat dwindled in size in exactly the same proportion and were still fitting him nicely. The old lady bent down with an effort, picked up the now-tiny Boris, who was waving his match-like hands frantically, and put him in the side pocket of her loose floor-length sarafan, on which stars and pentagrams were embroidered.

The audience gasped, not knowing whether to scream with fear or to applaud. The old woman went up to the microphone and pushed the stand down to match her height.

"Don't worry, ladies and gentlemen. He will shortly be back to his normal size and calibre too!" she announced in a calm and unexpectedly pleasant manner, with a touch of gentle irony. "But before it happens, let me assure you that I would have never dared interfere with the performance, had it not been made necessary by some truly extreme circumstances..."

"Who are you??" someone from the audience shouted.

On hearing this question, the old lady winced visibly, and her wrinkled face twitched as if with a sudden pang of toothache. "I beg you, ladies and gentlemen, to stop asking me direct questions. Due to an ancient curse I've been suffering from, each question makes me a wee bit older and adds another wrinkle to my face. So please, please, watch it, unless you want me to expire right here, in front of your eyes..."

"No, we don't!" several voices shouted.

"It is very kind of you, and we can now carry on with the performance," smiled the old lady. "My real name is not that important, but you can call me Yadwiga, if you wish. And my Cat here is called Bulgakov..."

Having heard his name, the Cat, who was still standing on his hind legs, began bowing ceremoniously left, right and centre – to the audience's delight.

"You may now be tempted to ask me where I am from and what brings me to Edinburgh – those popular British questions. Before you can do so, I am happy to reply that both my Cat and I come from two places simultaneously – Slavonia and Yesterdayland, the first being a country in Eastern Europe and the second – a peculiar space, or a dimension, if you wish, which is one day behind your normal time. I was known as Baba Yaga, or a yagishna, while living there. Yesterdayland also had some connections with Bookland – a domain populated by literary characters. One of the reasons that brought me to Edinburgh is trying to find my sister who has been missing from my life for nearly six hundred years."

Her last words were met with boos from the audience.

"I don't blame you for not believing me," Yadwiga continued. "Well, perhaps our little demonstration will make you more open-minded…"

"You choose what to show them, Bulgakov!" she said to the Cat.

"As my famous brother Behemoth, who was a great performer, used to say, let's do something simple first." He lifted his front paws above his head. "We are here to fulfill some of your dreams. By that I do not mean living up to the time when Scotland's football team defeated Brazil 10 to 1, for no magic in the world is capable of achieving that…"

"Haud on, mukker!" screamed someone from the third row. "Enough talking. Coorie up and do sum magic!"

"Awrite, awrite! Ho ye! A'm sairy!" replied the Cat in impeccable Old Scots. "Just wanted to establish what you, nice people of Edinburgh, are truly concerned about…"

"Pandas!" shouted another voice from the audience.

"Pandas? I think I know what you mean," said Bulgakov. "Correct me if I am wrong, but you must be talking about the two giant pandas, Tian Tian and Yang Guang, now dwelling in the Edinburgh Zoo. They like their food and – to everyone's annoyance – are not too willing to make cubs… Ae moment, please – I am going to sort it out once and for all – ane, twa, three!"

He jumped up in the air and gave out a long and loud hiss: "Sh-sh-sh-sh-sh!!"

A dozen or so black-and-white panda cubs appeared on stage out of nowhere. Having stood up on their hind legs, they joined together their fluffy front paws, formed a circle and started waddling around Yadwiga and Bulgakov in a sort of a *horovod* – a traditional Slavonic round dance.

"Oh-oh-oh!" breathed out the audience, ready to weep with emotion, but before they could do so the panda cubs let go of each other's paws. Having turned several synchronous somersaults, they rolled into one large black-and-white furry ball, out of which emerged one truly giant panda bear. He appeared at least ten feet tall when he stood on his hind legs. For a minute or so he was motionless, just standing there and staring at the audience, his large brown eyes with long eyelashes blinking benignly. Then he opened his mouth, said very clearly: "Zai Jian!!" and exploded silently, vanishing without a trace in the blinding glare of stage lights...

It was now the audience's turn to explode. In all its history the Royal Lyceum Theatre had never heard such a storm of applause. Even stage workers appeared from behind the scenes and were clapping their hands for all they were worth.

"Bravo! Bravo! Encore!"

The Cat was basking in glory – bowing to all sides and repeating: "Thenk ye! Thenk ye!"

"Bulgakov, stop clowning, will you?" that was Yadwiga coming up to the microphone again.

"Well, I can see that you have warmed up to us a wee bit," she said. "Warmth – this is what Edinburgh residents need desperately, both the people and the pandas, who might be more willing to procreate in a warmer climate. Warmth and sunlight... Such a lovely city: beautiful architecture, lots of history and culture – it's only the weather that keeps letting you down. Cold, rain and constant darkness can drive anyone mad... But let's try and change all that – even if for a short while!"

She closed her eyes, lifted both hands high above her head and chanted – loudly and clearly: "MINA PICA FRASCO!" And then again: "MINA PICA FRASCO!"

A strange-looking rider suddenly materialized in front of the audience. His face was red, he was dressed in red, and he rode a muscular crimson horse. Having galloped across the stage, he suddenly disappeared, as if he had sunk into the floor.

What followed exceeded the most far-reaching expectations. The walls and the roof of the theatre started crumbling apart slowly, with all the rubble evaporating before it reached the floor. Within a minute or so, the spectators found themselves sitting in the open air – fully exposed to the elements which on this occasion were represented by the ubiquitous Edinburgh drizzle falling from the habitually satin-grey skies. It was early evening in July and still light, if dull and overcast. While those who sat in the stalls tried to cover their heads with Festival programmes, the rain suddenly stopped and a hot blazing disc of the sun rose above the city, its Georgian streets now lined with plants, cedars and palm trees, instead of habitual limes, birches and poplars.

From their seats some of the spectators could now see as far as the Firth of Forth, yet from a considerable distance they were unable to discern the amazing changes to the waterfront, which had become a vast sandy beach, and to the bay itself, whose water was no longer opaque and dirty-grey but aquamarine and translucent, with sunlight reflected on its inviting wavy surface.

The most amazing transformation, however, was affecting the members of the audience whose black and brown trench-coats and sweaters, raincoats and mackintoshes – Edinburghers' habitual all-seasons attire – were replaced with skimpy bikinis and colourful swimming suits…

The change was so swift that there wasn't enough time to express surprise or to react in any other natural way. The spectators sat in complete silence, their mouths agape, and stared at each other in utter disbelief. They didn't even notice how the heavy and squeaky fold-up seats underneath them had become canvas-lined comfy beach chairs in which they were now reclining…

The whole city, which now looked and felt like a tropical resort, came to a stunned stand-still, all traffic stopped. Only soft rustling of surf against the sand, chirping of cicadas and piercing, almost human, screams of sea-gulls could be heard from the distance…

57207543R00121

Made in the USA
Charleston, SC
08 June 2016